# Avalon

# BY  S L DIXON

# AVALON

## S L DIXON

S L Dixon

ISBN:149297112X
ISBN-13: 978-1492971122

This small book will not change the world.

Instead it will invite you into another.

# ACKNOWLEDGMENTS

As a first time self-published author, releasing this book has required a great deal of help from close friends and family.

Firstly, I would like to thank my Grandmother Irene Nicholson for patiently sitting with me to edit this book, without her help the mistakes would have been tenfold.

I also must thank Nichola Cowley, Lesley Bell, Laura Bell and Compton McDonald for giving me the confidence I needed to pursue writing.

I would also like to thank my parents for their continued support in all aspects of my life.

Jade Edwards, thank you for your friendship over the last 10 years – more decades to come!

Last but not least I would like to thank Laura Hutchinson for her incredible cover design, capturing the essence of Avalon perfectly.

Finally I must thank you for taking the time to read this book, Avalon and the characters within in it have aided me through some challenging times.

I hope Avalon can do the same for you.

Welcome to my world.

# CONTENTS

# PROLOGUE

I have often found myself pondering the subject of beginnings, more specifically my own. My childhood wasn't exactly what you would call traditional or conventional; at least I never thought so for one my father certainly had not read the handbook on childcare and to be honest I think that even if a guide book had existed. He would have found several ways to undermine all the set guidelines and requirements regarding childcare. Aside from our DNA and dimples in our cheeks the only defining traits he and I had in common was that we both found facing up to certain responsibilities outside of work to be a challenging obligation - to say the least. Financially my father has always pulled through for me and my sister, it only took me to take refuge in another world to make me appreciate being at home.

I was never the only love in my father's rather unimaginative life for as long as I can remember his commitment to work reaped far greater rewards than could be found in any aspect of parenting. Which always made me question what compelled him to bring a life into a world in which this child would never be truly wanted in the first place, but we all make errors in judgement at one point or another.

My father works tirelessly at the cities top law firm in the centre of town, he has always been absolutely obsessed with justice. Not to mention the rewards that come with maintaining such a high profile competitive job. We never really saw much of him over the space of a week, my father didn't cope very well with losing a case.

Not that it mattered, he celebrated winning and losing the exact same way with a truck load of expensive imported beer. He would always compensate his absence with gifts and surprise holidays a few times a year, but even a getaway wasn't a good enough distraction. His mind was never far *enough* away from the job. Constantly seeking out the next high profile case in which he could make the biggest amount of money was his obsession.

The bright star in my otherwise clear childhood sky was Alice who fell into her own wonderland, which was both utterly outrages and undeniably hypnotic. Of course she woke to find the entire thing had been nothing greater than a figment of her wild adolescent imagination. I often wondered what would of happened if it hadn't been a dream; would she have spent her limitless youth immersed in the amazing world? Or would she have rather been at one with reality and what exactly was her reality?

I know I would have stayed within the dream because let's face it everything is better than reality, right?

What about Jack and his beanstalk, James and his giant peach, me and my kingdom.

Let's imagine for a moment that things never devolved into an endless battle of good vs. evil. It's astonishing to comprehend the endless possibilities that could be accomplished if we had nothing to fight against. Just like the death of the wicked witch in The Wizard of Oz, would everything in this world suddenly change? Would the world be a brighter place? Could I at last get permission for my prince to join me in my tower?

So many unanswered questions.

AVALON

When I was much younger and much less wiser I never thought that maybe my mother had a point in saying, I should get my head out of the fairy tale books. Each of them apparently filled with goblins and various 'literary lies.' But when you're a mere twelve years old and your father is an absent workaholic; it's fair to say that you needed something to entertain and distract you, during the mandatory weekly visits to his new apartment. His escape situated conveniently two minutes away from the court house. He'd been warned a few times about falling asleep in his office chair after hours, so the apartment became his second home.

Most of the time he was too tired to drive the twenty miles back to the family home so, against my mother's wishes he bought a grotty two bedroom apartment. He returned home two or 3 times a week to spend the night with his family, burring my head in the land of boundless make-believe was a welcome escape from my mother's constant worrying.

Years before everything became so completely out of control my work driven father and I would take refuge in the local bar, again around the corner from his new place. After a few visits I became accustomed to the uncomfortable seats, his rowdy colleagues, the stale smell of beer and cigarettes. The awful aroma combination had been absorbed into every stick of worn out second hand furniture, all crammed into the relatively small bar.

The jukebox would chime out hits from decades gone by, Otis Redding was my favourite artist on the playlist. My father gave me money to play him on repeat whilst he rambled on and on about work. Never anything confidential of course, he mainly ranted about his colleagues. He was ever so completive if he could bet in accordance to court cases outcome, he would.

In preparation for these nights out he spent hundreds of pounds on tailor made suits and parties with his upper class boorish friends. The more he drank at these parties,

3

the more convinced he became that his next case was an impending victory, already spending his winnings. It was a vicious endless circle which always ended the same way walking home without a single pound in his back pocket.

The décor in his two bedroom rented shoddy apartment was worse than the pub; it was so different to the family home I had grown up in. This was his place and it hadn't been cleaned since he moved in. It was only after I'd stayed over one night to spend more time with him that I realised he was leading two completely parallel lives. The apartment was a contrast to the pristine state of my parents' home. Its squeaky clean condition was purely down to the dedication of my mother, a complete perfectionist when it came to household maintenance.

In the rented apartment the dark carpets had devolved into a crusty thick layer of dirt beneath my trainers, the landlord didn't seem to have the money to add some homely touches. The bedroom was just a mount of worn clothing heaped into a pile ready to take over to my mother's for a good wash and a mandatory ironing.

The hideous netting which hung like a spider's web at the windows, everything had been stained with various shades of yellow from the previous tenants smoking too close to the windows worn wooden frame. In the early hours my father would still be sat up rereading through his clients information in preparation for the following day, whilst I ate the leftovers from the night before.

On returning home, I knew it was better to keep the evenings events from my pretentious mother. She certainly wasn't fond of my father's colleagues, none of them were particularly faithful to their wives, opening gloating about dating other women. My father wasn't a cheater, he just enjoyed the witty banter of being with the boys. What my mother couldn't understand  was that when my father was free from beneath her thumb he was finally able to relax. Allowing us the time to sit in peace in the middle of the draftee living room and write comical and often meaningful lyrics on the back of old newspapers.

Having this quality time made the time spent in the pub and his awful apartment worth every minute. Whenever we wrote together my father would beam with a delirious pride at what we had accomplished. After a while though my mother grew tired of my father's parties with his friends and the visits to my father's apartment became less frequent. She gave him no choice but to return home more often to spend time with his children.

In my mother's presence my father was a completely different man, not a trace of his party side in sight. He cooked, did all the dishes and he even helped with the laundry. It was only when he was left to his own devices that things became a little messy.

Till this day, I don't think my mother has ever given me half the amount of attention or showed a fraction of the pride as my father did on those weekends. Amelia was always her favourite, she's older than me, the first born. I guess my mother didn't have much left to offer after donating so much of her time to Amelia.

The more mature I become the more I am beginning to understand that in every fragmented stage of this life, we will all be tested in one way or another and it all starts with school. The poorly maintained buildings with patchy unpainted brick walls, large corridors and frightfully huge halls played host to my first official steps onto the ladder leading up to adulthood.

My mother ran her own cookery business teaching novices and she even managed to get a slot on day time TV in her early years, now she creates recipe books and manages a very popular online blog.

With mortgage payments and university fees to think about my family opted out of sending me to a private school. Naively I was still filled with hope and expectations fed to me by my favourite American films and sitcoms, of a school filled with happy cheerful children.

In the few days leading up to my first day, I quickly became host to the more traditional worries that come with joining any social or educational convention. Such as physical appearance and trying desperately to avoid being the subject of fictitious malicious gossip, which spread like a wildfire beneath a blazing Caribbean sun.

I slowly found out that I harboured an inability to make friends, with morally truthful people my own age. I always seemed to be drawn towards those in my year who had their own hidden agendas.

In the morning my mother would make me a packed lunch and every afternoon I would sit in a toilet cubical, trying to make as little noise as possible as I ate the generous contents of it. Of course there was always a chance a persistent hall monitor would realise the same toilet door had been locked for a while. My hiding place was almost always uncovered, it was either that or try to find a seat in the crowded cafeteria.

I always came to the conclusion that being found in the bathroom would be less embarrassing and easier to explain then the torturous humiliation that came with being denied a spot at the popular table, during the lengthy lunch hour.

Back then I was convinced that physical education was just a subject devised between teachers and popular students. To degrade people like me and by people like me, I mean the more physically challenged of us. In an attempt to escape the hour long lesson I would accidently forget my kit but this little trick didn't work out exactly as I had planned.

The short grey haired teacher had a navy blue box in her small untidy office, jam-packed with grubby clothing that had been left behind from the pupils who graduated the year earlier. I was forced to pick some out and wear that instead not only was the smell revolting but nothing fit me which meant tirelessly clutching to them whilst I tried to participate in the lesson. The footwear I was given to wear made my feet resemble those of a clown ,as if the lesson wasn't embarrassing enough. I had to do it while dressed like an uncoordinated idiot, more of an idiot than usual that is. From that day on I never forgot my kit again.

I never had any real motivation to succeed throughout school, during the 4 years that I was subjected to the lessons; I can just about remember my mother attending two of the numerous parent's evenings, at which my academic progress was under the microscope.

Let's just say, I was never worried about the teachers claiming I talked too much in class. In my busy mother's defence she attended more meetings than my constantly absent father.

After great internal deliberation I am now very much glad that Tyler had attended a different school then I did, at the time I was certainly not ready for him to come into my still juvenile life. Keeping up relationships at such a young tender age must be difficult but increasingly so when you have so many testing and forever evolving circumstances to deal with.

Another test I'm still trying to conquer is finding my identity; I have never been able to relate to those people who toward the end of high school already had their paths mapped out. Already having an idea of the kind of person they wanted to be, the career and the lifestyle they wanted.

I'm proud to say the tables have turned around considerably.

I suppose I'm telling you this to let you know things were not always like this. I wasn't always the strong woman you are about to see as my story unravels.

I certainly did not wake up one day with buckets full of boundless courage and wild determination on my doorstep. Everything you see here is a product of my troubled past, but let me tell you this. If I have learnt anything along the way it's that the future is definitely worth the fight.

The future is yours to mould and conquer; the only person who could stop you from living an extraordinary life is you. I had been given a normal childhood with all of its faults and rewards for a reason. I was later handed an exceptional adulthood from a life I never knew I had, from a world I never knew existed and from a family I never knew I needed.

This is not a rags to riches story, a romance or an action thriller. This is a story about what can happen if you never give up, if you never put limitations on your own strength, and you always cling to hope. Let me begin by telling you about my great grandmother as without her I never would have inherited the path I now walk on.

Until the end she was forever whispering words of wisdom though her pale, fragile and honest lips she would so often tell me that our personal possessions were just that personal. Explaining that the life we are given is never scripted in stone it is our right to make changes, alteration after alteration.

She believed without question that the items we possess hold within them a fraction of ourselves over time. She told me that when a person no longer had need for the possession it still holds something of its owner indefinitely.

She would clutch her own pendant which lay at the nape of her neck with a smile; she believed a part of her was imprinted on that pendant like a permanent fingerprint.

So you can only imagine my apprehension once it was given to me at the wake of her passing, the fear of misplacing it was passionate. The moment it was positioned at the nape of my neck I swore it would remain there.

For safe keeping.

# AVALON

# PREFACE

As we all marched in perfectly executed synchronicity towards absolute ambiguity the screams were deafening. The overrun territory was alive with intruders as violent and deadly bolts of blacked electricity darted in every direction. Striking repeatedly through the air as though sent from angry merciless gods; momentarily obstructing our view of the once glorious chambers, holding within it both the souls of brave and treacherous beings. If you accidently blinked you might just have missed the repetitive blasts. "Be brave." I whispered to myself just "Be brave." But no matter how many times I reiterated the mantra to myself, my scrawny knees kept on shaking, my palms kept on sweating and she kept on running towards me.

Between snarling lips her sharp teeth continued clenching and snapping together. She was ready to tear me to shredded lumps of meat, dangerously close to my petrified pale face. Until inevitably her avaricious hands wrapped around my vulnerable throat, my palpitating pulse pounding against her cold fingers. I trapped a swell of air between my lungs hoping it would give me a few extra seconds of consciousness. My eyes staring at the orange blood which coated every part of her ravenous body. Her red dress exhibited the stains of her weaker less fortunate victims, *so many* that I had to close my eyes to stop myself from plucking a very plausible number of victims out of thin air.

In these diminishing moments I began to hear his charming voice, as though he was stood beside me. Screaming a message of strength louder and louder beside my listening ears, furiously demanding I fight not allowing my exhausted bones to wilt and shatter beneath me. His words guided me to the untapped power within me, finally I found the courage to lift my sluggish foot from under me and with one brutal unrelenting blow to her solid abdomen she was propelled to smithereens and with that my skin was no longer host to the residue from her frothing starved mouth. This was only the beginning. The start of what was to be a vicious and heart plundering conclusion.

I fell hard against the cold pavement the cement instantly crumbling beneath at the mercy of the abrupt force. My knees did not surrender to the sudden impact I had finally found my way home, his bedroom light flickering between the partitions of his closed curtains swaying in the breeze. I could just about hear the monotonous back and forth ramblings of his family, his face formed a block between my delusions and indefinite reality.

This man would one day risk his life to bring mine back from the brink but of course I didn't know that yet.

The only promise regularly enforced in life is that one day it will end in my exclusively mortal existence. I took comfort in the understanding that we were all headed in the same direction. Now that I had ridden this world of one of its greatest evils, had this action granted me privileges or sanctions?

Final thoughts rattled around my head like a bee trapped inside a thick drinking glass desperate to find a way out, and failing repeatedly.

# 1. REMORSE

"What am I going to do with you?" I answered his condescending question as a grin grew on his flawless kissable just licked lips

"Well... You could always leave me to this fate; you do know that I'm not expecting you to stick around to endure my inevitable self-deprecating and potentially hazardous endeavours, right?"

His enchanting green eyes lowered in response to my overly cavalier uncharacteristic response I tried my best to think of a different topic something less controversial; the weather? His new car? The shelf I needed him to straighten?

I was desperate for a topic changer regardless of its insignificant nature but before I was given the chance to speak, his finger was placed over my lips silencing me.

"Now you listen to me."

His words were resilient but his tone remained light and playful as he layered the tough love on extra thick today, much to my humbled amusement.

"I love you. You have so much to offer that your eyes won't let you see let me offer you my eyes Miss, you already have my heart. Now see what I see. You have the soul of a warrior, not to mention the courage and determination of a lioness."

He grinned brightly, caressing my crimson cheek with his soft fingertips as he continued to speak.

"You Eva are everything to me no matter what may or may not happen. You know better than anyone that I don't make promises easily but I am willing to promise you myself, for as long as you want me, mark or no mark."

His beautiful smirk glorified his extravagant words and to be honest with you, I shouldn't have been too surprised, he had always been prone to generous hales of affection. I couldn't never help the array embarrassed blushes which would always follow his undeserved complements. At a time like this, I knew I was lucky to be receiving them.

Tyler was handsome, who am I kidding, Tyler was without a doubt the most beautiful person I had ever met. His eyes hold within them an assortment of dark tones, warm hazelnut with a slight golden caramel undertone.

Unlike me he was tanned and always looked like he had just returned from a vacation not unlike his brother. They both caught the sun ridiculously easy, I on the other hand burn to a bright red crisp whenever the sun set its eyes on me.

I'm in love with this beautiful man, to whom I usually confided in about everything but had decided not to tell him about the two unbearable choices I needed to make. No matter how much I tried to choose between them I couldn't, recent extraordinary circumstances were about to lead me down a path I was destined to follow. A path which more specifically was about to lead me away from here. Away from this life and away from him indefinitely.

His dexterous fingers began to rhythmically stroke the marking which had expanded further along my underarm, since I acquired it a mere few  days ago. Its ever increasing growth was the very least of my mounting problems.

I clung to the soft blue polyester that was Tyler's shirt, I cowered in his protective and always open arms as he began to fall asleep. I allowed my mind to wonder in an ambitious attempt to distract myself from the impending ending of our previously peaceful relationship.

I knew I needed to leave this house but my head, my legs and my feet would not comply. I needed just a few additional minutes with him, just a few more milliseconds of undivided, unrestricted and totally unforgettable embraces. If our love was fire; we were rapidly running out of oxygen.

If I put this off the inevitable any longer, I would never find the strength to leave.

Being around Tyler was easy, I loved him enough to supress my new twisted desires. The very thought of being in the company of strangers was terrifying, the hunger wasn't so bad right now. But I had seen what this life can do to you over time, I had seen Julia. This disease of sorts was courtesy of the prolific woman in red.

This new way of existing which had been forced upon me required such great substance, it was overwhelming. I knew that in order to quench the blistering thirst I would ultimately have to sacrifice everything I had built up in this mortal life, including myself.

I knew all too well how fatal one wrong move could be. I had fooled myself into thinking that craving him could be the antidote to potentially cure me from this hell. But the chance that my alternative needs would become too overwhelming in his presence was horrifying.

I could no longer force myself to pick between the two needs in my life, my new need to feed on everyone around me and my love for Tyler. The battle between my two desires had just begun and I couldn't face its consequences alone, not even Tyler could help me now.

The small compact mirror I placed in the compartment of my black heavyweight backpack, wouldn't let me forget. Nor would it let me escape what I had faced and what I was yet to go up against. I knew that if nothing else my reflection would always be a constant reminder of what I've been through.

These black poisoned eyes would always be those of a killer though I had not yet killed by choice, I will always be craving the rewards a kill can provide. Loathing the unquenchable desire as though it was an incurable sickness slowly eating away at my raging defenceless insides.

I'd stuffed all I could into my mother's rucksack; I didn't feel guilty for borrowing it without permission after all she never did use it. I guess you never really know how to prepare yourself for something totally foreign. So I grabbed a few essentials including a change of clothes, petty cash and my mobile phone. Anything additional would be merely materialistic.

I patiently but anxiously waited for my devoted Tyler to wake up, his tattooed sleeve peeping out from beneath our velvet cream sheets. Please allow me to take just another minuet of your time to tell you a little more about my knight in shining armour Mr Drayga.

Tyler is my very own share of ecstasy in an otherwise mundane existence. He was introduced to me at my sister Amelia's glamorous graduation party held at our house, when I had just turned sixteen, Tyler was my genius. He had graduated a year earlier than everyone else aged just seventeen, I had only gotten to know him briefly from an agonising distance.

If he wanted to Tyler could do so much better than me and I knew he could, if the truth be told so did everyone else. It was an unspoken statement written in bold across every disapproving face, whenever we went out publicly together.

"What on earth is such an excruciatingly handsome graduate doing with a girl who didn't know her left from her right?" They would whisper, I never did send any witty retorts their way.

When I also graduated Tyler sketched me the first portrait of what was to become a cherished collection. In true Tyler style instead of his signature at the bottom of his incredibly accurate drawing, he simply wrote a beautiful quote. From one of my biggest inspirations Mahatma Gandhi. "Live as if you were to die tomorrow. Learn as if you were to live forever."

Tyler added "And love as if we never had to say goodbye." With those words I was hooked.

Tyler and I both shared a love of literature, an obsessive love of music and an unrelenting great love for each other. I never thought a day would come in which I would be closing the door on a home which held so many memories of us. I began listening to the hands on the clock ticking as I waited for that painful moment to come.

The repetitive noise had become the only sound in an otherwise silent room, until his yawn startled me as he finally awakened. I smiled softly and took a seat at the end of the small bed, by now my heavy bag was placed over the shoulder of my dark brown overcoat.

I stared into his eyes as a tear fell down my cheek feeling the pain of the words I was yet to speak, I ran my finger along his defined jaw as he sat up to kiss my frowning brow. The gentle kiss soon had me relaxed my smile reflected his for what I was sure would be the last time; his curved lips had always been infections but not knowing if I would ever see it again resulted in my smile being unusually cut short.

My entire body began to tremble as the stream of tears seemed never ending, he must have assumed that I'd had yet another bad dream. Tyler wiped away droplet after droplet, his hand stinging as the venom laced liquid fell to his fingers and down to his wrist. His face never letting on to the combination of anguish and pain he must have been feeling beneath the surface. Before the change it wasn't an unusual occurrence for me to wake up with a tear stained pillow at the hands of a nightmare, I was so lucky to have him to wake up beside in those vulnerable moments.

It wasn't enough anymore, nothing he could say or do would sway my decision in his favour, I needed to do this. It wasn't until his hand reached out for mine that he came into contact with my black driving gloves. I clung to him as I would my last breath, savouring it and finally using it to whisper 'I love you'.

I felt his grip on my hand tighten now as if it represented his greater hold on me. I managed to pull my head from his chest long enough to kiss him delicately, it stopped him from answering any questions for just a moment.

It was a selfish indulgence to take the last kiss and use it as both a delay and a distraction but I knew no matter how long we kissed it would never be long enough. The kiss deepened as our lips moulded together until I felt his lungs straining for another breath. Before I knew it, I had to bring myself to explain that I was leaving for reasons I couldn't describe, for something he couldn't understand.

Tyler continued profusely requesting he accompany me until I was out the door, I tried reasoning but truthfully at the time I would have tied him to a chair if it would have stopped him from coming with me.

At least I could find comfort in the knowledge he was safe if nothing else, he may not have known it at the time but I was the only danger here. I was the predator hidden under a cloak he had provided for me.

I tried to brush away the cloud of pain that hung over my head as I he carried my rucksack to the back door. I couldn't bring myself to look into his eyes as mine would have told of much sorrow and even more of betrayal

"Just one week apart." I told both him and myself but deep down I knew it wasn't a commendable timescale more of an uneducated guess. The lie did however make his expression soften if nothing else I felt my slow palpitating heart beating against my rib cage as I simultaneously felt his eyes looking down on me. I placed another selfish kiss on his lips, I heard the closing of the front door before I had even reached my mini cooper. I guessed he couldn't bear to watch me leave; I knew that I deserved this aching feeling in the pit of my stomach, a grave sensation of bitter resentment toward myself erupted for putting him through this based on an improbability.

In my small efficient car I set off on my ridiculous adventure, gradually passing all the geographical representations of my childhood. First came the now boarded up school I attended, followed by the park where Tyler and I had our first date. Then the arena at which I had seen my first concert with my aunt and finally my grandmothers old house, which had certainly seen better days.

Now, it was just the road and buildings without any specific significance just bricks of varying decay all aligned together illuminated by the glare of the cities streetlights. I forced myself to look forward, visualising myself in the future with answers and a happier state of mind, these thoughts stopped me from turning my car around. I only put my foot on the break to fill up the penurious tank when the light on the dashboard flashed again and again;

I drove in silence intermittently glancing at the guidelines on the map on the passenger's seat beside me, the occasional road sign reminded me of the distance I had travelled. Eventually I pulled up at one of the many franchised roadside hotels all with neon signs beckoning me, I couldn't ignore them anymore. My sight had deteriorated to the point that I could no longer read the various road signs that were approaching, my eyes and mind had both become equally delirious with sleep deprivation.

I booked a standard room for the evening on the automated computerised check-in system at the reception desk, all the rooms were pretty basic with a beige colour scheme running throughout. Each room had the same selection of stained carpeted floors with an assortment of once decorative wallpaper which had begun to peal from the walls.

Room number 88 would be my sanctuary for the night and I was going to make the best of it, I tried to open the window to get rid of the stuffy aroma in the room but the wooden frame wouldn't budge. In the late hour it didn't take long for the poorly maintained TV to become mundane with various infomercials; the occasional dash of colour became the only thing which kept me distracted from staying solely inside my own fractured thoughts.

Even that small distraction couldn't stop sleep from its constant attempts to take me, it continued making my lids heavier with each passing minuet. As I closed my eyes I was reminded of the nightmares and the terrifying images which have eluded my dreams for the past few weeks. Each were hiding behind my eyelids ready to come to life the moment I dared to rest, I had lost all interest in sleep. In an attempt to fend off exhaustion for as long as I was able, I decided to give caffeine and sugary foods a try.

I dragged my feet along the cold floor putting on my grey slippers as I headed towards the elevator, just down the corridor from my room. I pressed the button impatiently as I waited for it to respond. I took in a heavy breath as my attention was grabbed by a young man stood nearby delivering food to the room just a few doors down from mine. I'd hadn't considered ordering food directly to my room but it seemed that the catering staff were the only team working 24/7.

I waited while he handed the woman some french fries and a giant bottle of cola. I smiled at him politely as he moved towards me in his baggy maroon uniform and black laced shoes. His face was pale as I licked my lips from what I thought was the scent of the french fries. I then realised it was no longer that aroma which appealed to me.

My throat ached and my stomach churned, keep it together Eva.

"Excuse me? I'm Eva, from room 88, I was wondering if I-"

Cutting my sentence short I narrowed my blisteringly tired eyes forcing them to focus as I followed his intense unwavering gaze. It was then that I looked down to my t-shirt expecting to see a collection of offensive words or a picture he could be processing just my blue sweats. Nothing which could provoke this uncomfortable stare from him and certainly nothing obviously conspicuous.

Looking up again he was tripping over his own feet I could hear his heartbeat thudding in my ears, the young man was riddled with fear as he continued to run so fast that he accidentally tripped again. He quickly vanished from my blurred view but his heartbeat was still a penetrating ring in my ear, I coiled back into the wall behind me as I did so I felt the bubble ridden wallpaper popping against my shoulders as I continued slouching down it.

Holding my head in my hands it was at that moment that I caught sight of my mark it had been peeking out from under my short sleeved top it couldn't possibly be the reason why he ran, could it?

My mind raced with wicked questions as I yanked down my sleeve and I ran back to my room. I slammed my room key into the slot twisting and retracting it forcefully; I accidentally crushed the rusting door handle in my sweating hand in my rush to get back to solitude. Slamming the door shut behind me taking a breath as my fickle knees buckled under me again.

*'Nothing happened, he wasn't running from you, you controlled yourself well done.'*

A few hours had passed but I could still taste the desire lurking on the roof of my mouth as much as I wanted to talk myself out of it. I should probably sleep this off; I needed to do something to replenish myself with a bit of luck I wouldn't have any more episodes or interruptions. I don't know how much longer I can subdue myself from the delight that is a strangers vulnerability.

I tried my damnedest to give myself a rest that night, keeping myself locked in the confines of the dingy hotel room underneath the stiff paper like blanket on the small uncomfortable bed. I didn't have cause to complain, it was ultimately all I could afford and it was certainly an improvement on last nights' accommodation curled up in the back seat of my car. The radio playing and the heating working intermittently compared to that, this was a 5 star all inclusive hotel.

The small collection of complimentary goods were a god send, I scrubbed every inch of myself in the shower. I ran a comb through my conditioned hair until every long strand was in place, I really could do with having it trimmed the ends were beginning to feel a little frayed.

After a hot shower and an all-round clean up, I wrapped up in a white cotton towel taking a seat at the small vanity unit at the corner of the room. I squeezed the ends of my hair letting the droplets of cold water fall onto the towel. I made myself a sweet cup of tea using the small sachets provided as I took a sip and picked up the local newspaper

'The Toucan Times.' As I flicked through it I really did feel like a tourist, page after page of articles about places I didn't know. Full of faces I didn't recognise and names I couldn't identify. After a quick glance at the business section I found myself searching through the few job vacancies in the area mostly remedial work, I sighed.

If I don't find whatever the hell I was holding out for then I might need this, I tore out the section and added it to my pile of goods I still needed to pack away. I tossed the paper back onto the counter and reluctantly met the gaze of my reflection thinking about my future. I suppose could have a desk job, or better yet, work from home, I would need total isolation. I chocked at the prospect of complete segregation and then realised that if I couldn't get myself under some sort of rational control, I'd never be happy or safe around members of the public.

"What am I going to do with my life?" I had barely finished college and I don't have much of a life to go back to. "I need to keep moving forward." I kept reminding myself.

I packed some of the hotels goods into my already stuffed full bag but it wasn't long until I became increasingly aware that the sound I was hearing was no longer that of the radio which had woken me this morning. I swear the stupid thing did not have an off button, from 7am this morning it hadn't stopped. I had been fazing in and out of the enthusiastic presenters' inane chatter and loud music, all laced with a heavy base which had led to my head pounding along to the beat. Not even the radio could drown out the intimidating voices erupting from the other side of my closed hotel door.

The deep male voices talking about reviewed CCTV footage and an impending visit from News Crews, channels 1, 3, 5 and 7... It was then that reality hit - it was as if a truck just slammed into me at an unstoppable speed and I could feel every inch of the insatiable impact hitting my body. They were talking about me at that moment a huge lump formed in my dry throat as the yelling was becoming more antagonistic. Threatening to enter if I did not wilfully open the door. The only thing between me and them was about 5 inches of poorly constructed wood and a rusted old door handle

I groaned as it was relentlessly tested from the other side. The legends here turned out to be more than just stories, the people of this town were damn near obsessed with vampire stories and tales alike, only I could choose a place like that to stay for the night.

Leaving via the nearest fire exit wasn't exactly the most dignified departure. The only sound I was able to hear as I retreated to my car was the fire alarm which I must have triggered in my haste to leave the building. Lord only knows why I chose to park in the furthest spot away from the exit., but I suppose this wasn't exactly how I planned to check out of the hotel. I threw my backpack onto the passenger's seat jamming the key into the ignition, the engine roaring to life as soon as I turned the key.

I hated this; I hated that I already had restrictions and rules over circumstances which I could no longer control, such as living like a convict who has been wrongly accused in the eyes of everyone I have come into contact with. I was just trying to prevent being captured by those vultures all waiting for a chance to peck at my now quirked brain with their medical journals and inevitable list of unanswerable questions. At least not when I had an endless collection of my own unresolvable questions to ask a ghost.

Living out of my small mini cooper did however have its perks though; it made for much needed easy getaways which I now knew would prove essential for my voyage into the unknown. If only I had opted for an upgrade a few months earlier for a mini countryman rather than my black mini convertible, how appropriate that improvement could have been. I pulled down the sun shade to protect my eyes from the morning sun. Just as soon as the car was in gear I drove away from the chaos.

# 2. FEAR, DANGER AND SOPHISTICATED MEN

I knew my destination wouldn't be present on the road map which my sister had jokingly bought me for my 18th birthday last year. Along with my poor navigational skills it seemed that every road started to merge into one continuous stretch. It wasn't until my car stalled on the third night that I really felt utterly misplaced and helpless without Tyler beside me.

At such a time like this having Tyler around would have been appreciated. I stopped that painful thought before I let it claw at the still open wound. I managed to push the car to the side of the winding vacant motorway just far enough so that it was out of sight. I have to admit I was a little smug at my strength, luckily no one was around to question it.

It didn't take long for it to dawn on me just how remote this stretch of road was, in my own neighbourhood you couldn't walk down the street without the possibility of bumping into all different walks of life, far too often in fact. But here, you could walk for miles without as much as a single disruption, I'll never get used to that.

I collected a few essentials from the stuffed boot and crammed as much as I could into every compartment of my already exasperated backpack. I then tightened the frayed laces on my now filthy trainers and pulled up the hood of my winter coat to shield myself from the rain which blasted down from the black clouds hovering above me, as I hit the road.

I suppose the walk wasn't completely without interruption I did need to keep checking my step every time a huge truck passed by in order for me to jump out of the way to avoid getting drenched further, by the large pools of water gathering by the side of the road.

I kept my cold hands around the straps of my backpack as I strode along the ominous highway the more time that passed by my decision to travel off road became a necessity. The roads had quickly transformed into a swarm of motorcycles, loud obnoxious horns and impatient engines revving with annoyance at the humongous traffic ques.

I found that nothing *even here* stays tranquil for very long.

The early morning rush had begun and the more I thought about it I knew it was inevitable that I would eventually have no other choice but to ditch my car. I couldn't afford to keep my cars tank topped up. I couldn't bare the idea of making a desperate call to my father to beg him wire me some additional funds. I knew he would only agree so long as I turned myself around and I wasn't ready to do that just yet. I wonder if he even realised I was missing.

The trees, the serene hills and beautiful mountains in the distance drew me I like a moth to a flame and right now I was a very willing moth. I found myself delighted by even the quietest crunch of broken branches beneath my feet. The peaceful harmony of light winter winds disturbing the uncut fields of flowers, grass and weeds became my safe haven from the hard foot paths and stretches of angry motorists. Here I could walk between the trees for hours... I had been walking for hours.

My aching knees and shoulders cried out for a moment of reprieve. I dropped the backpack which felt like a ton of bricks onto the acorn covered ground, I began rummaging through the compartments of the overworked carrier; my body willingly slumped against the patterned bark of an old oak tree, taking a much needed gulp of concentrated cranberry juice from the water bottle I had topped up at the hotel. I devoured the sugary snacks and breakfast bars I bought from the last aesthetically abandoned gas station off the highway I had visited.

Physically I don't know how much more of this adventure I can take. If it wasn't for the symbol on my arm and my desire to seek revenge I wouldn't choose to go any further. After all I wasn't following a map nor was I heading in any particular direction, my instincts were leading me now. Instincts which I felt were taking over me completely, the path ahead was already willing me forward.

I forced myself back up onto my feet it seemed like it had been only a few hours since I watched the enthralling pink and orange sunrise beaming down over the motorway - where had the rest of the day gone?

When working at my father's law firm over the summer period to earn some extra money, I can never remember the days ever feeling this tediously short.

It didn't take me long to realise the vines of the trees above me couldn't provide enough protection against the elements as the rain persisted. Upon standing up I brushed off my jeans and adjusted my hood as I once again put one foot in front of the other. As I marched forever forward I was astonished to see that the pendant which hung from around my neck had begun to glow a beautiful pale ocean blue. It had never done that before, my eyes darted to the sky to catch a glace of what it could be reflecting much to my dismay the skies were still grey, was I hallucinating?

The greater the distance I journeyed the brighter and more potent the colour became aside from the huge moon which shone intermittently between the breaks in the clouds, the pendant became my only source of light as the black night took provenance.

It was here, buried deep in the sweltering woods that I was startled by another traveller. Apart from the hotel incident he was the first person I had come across since Tyler on a face to face basis. I was almost relieved at the prospect of company - even of a total stranger. I was starting to think I was on the verge of losing my mind.

The man however was a shady character with penetrating eyes and charcoal smoothed skin. He might as well have leaped down from the overhanging trees startling me with his unannounced arrival. I kept my distance as much as I was starved for some normal conversation but this man didn't appear to be the conversational type.

From a distance he continued to follow me with an intimidatingly leering stance, I tried relentlessly to walk on seeking out suitable shelter. He wasn't doing a good job of remaining inconspicuous the man seemed irritatingly determined to get my attention. His footing was careful as he kept to slightly higher ground just behind me, he never questioned his next step - the man was incredibly smooth, too smooth. If it wasn't for the sound of his broad shoulders brushing against crackling dead leaves I would never have known he was there *lurking*. I had no idea exactly how long he'd been following me.

Eventually and reluctantly I met his intrusive expectant gaze, despite my best efforts he couldn't keep his eyes off my pendant. In an attempt to distract the tall loitering man I gripped the pendant in my hand as I began to speak, shielding it from his gaze, giving him no other option than to meet my equally intrusive stare.

"Is there something I can do for you? Don't you know it's rude to stare? Or is all common courtesy lost on you?"

He glared at me as my cold tone had slashed his ideals of the woman he perhaps thought he knew. His face revealing the angered words he was keeping to himself. Nevertheless he shook his head changing his expression into one of abrupt confidence. It took me a few seconds to notice he was traveling without a great deal of luggage which led me to think he hadn't travelled far, there must be a town or motel nearby either of which would be a blessing. I grinned at the thought of finally being able to take this weight off my exhausted legs.

After what seemed to be a long and awkward silence, the man began to speak - he never did answer my questions, he simply replied with...

"Greetings Miss Evangeline A Carter, it's a pleasure."

I watched him with a questioning and bemused expression as you can imagine. He didn't appear to hold the trademarks of anyone I had ever met. I was relentlessly trying to place him from memory or from a page from my scrupulous research. With no success I asked with less patience filtering through my tone.

"I'm sorry, have we met?" His warped grin grew at my snappy retort *he* was enjoying this, bathing in my utter confusion; his reaction instantly placed an uneasy feeling in the pit of my empty stomach.

"Not officially." His tone was as smooth as his footsteps, the deep calm tone of his words had relaxed my shoulders and slowed my previously frightful heart. As soon as he spoke those suggestive words, he began walking towards me, offering his bandaged grey cloth covered hand to mine. Immediately I shook it firmly then diverted back to gazing at his fascinating ever changing eyes, constantly altering from one bright colour to the next as he spoke, I couldn't keep myself from staring. They transformed from a startling maroon to a beautiful turquois then a summer grass green in seconds.

I'd once read somewhere that a handshake can reveal so much about you on the first encounter, if I was ever going to stand a chance at figuring out what the hell had happened to me this was surely it. I needed to make a good impression, to prove I was ready for whatever he had been searching for. I needed this, please god let this be it. I kept my wits about me as the conversation continued.

"It's Eva actually and will you please clarify what you meant by not officially."

I couldn't stop my prying investigative eyes from scanning his unusual attire, undeterred and completely unprovoked by my unmasked brash adolescent attitude; he spoke with precise eloquent fluidity.

"You dear are something of a legend in these parts, a myth if you'd like but I'm no fool. I would recognise you anywhere. I must apologise I haven't formally introduced myself, I am Hedwinn Lord of the forgotten but not lost kingdom of AVALON'!"

I stared at him blankly, stubbing my foot into the ground and nodding solemnly.

"Right..? That explains it." I laughed sheepishly as I came to the very rapid conclusion he was a man very much not of the right mind. He's under the illusion that he is the leader of some made up secret organisation. As I stepped back he looked at me with a less then amused expression. Finally he took in one deep breath sensing my anxiety then smiled.

"I've been sent here to collect you." He cast his eyes around the unusually quiet and darkening woods, before looking back in my direction.

"I will lead you to where you belong - the whole colony is waiting for you. Wouldn't want to keep them waiting now would we?"

It was as though all my matured adult judgment had escaped my conscious mind, as I stepped toward him he responded with a confident grin before leading us deeper into the livening forest. In an effort to justify my unintelligible actions, I knew I wasn't getting anywhere alone wandering in circles probably, so I thought I would humour him.

It wasn't until I noticed a hidden mark under his bandaged hand identical to my own that I knew he could be serious. Maybe there was a chance his claims could contain some potential for the truth, or had I lost my mind too?

The mark was an exact replica to the one Julia had scarred me with, what if he was being truthful?

Perhaps a world that was a complete blind spot to the rest of society really could exist, a haven for those like me, the thought of which overwhelmed me and at last gave me a sense of relief.

I thought back to my experience with Julia after all she was the one who had subjected me to this. She tore me away from the love of my life, my family and if the books from my research were anything to go by she had slashed away part of my soul; Julia too bared the same hideous mark, just on a different place on her body.

Hedwinn was so different to the stereotype I had come to associate with the people whose branding matched mine. He exuded such positive yet contagious energy with gentle eyes and a kind domineer. I knew for sure he was trustworthy, at least enough for me to let him lead me into the ibis. I was admittedly rather nervous in his presence my past relationships with male dominant figures usually ended up in a clash of options of sorts, I was keeping a reasonable distance remaining consciously careful when we exchanged conversation.

Finally we pitched up beside a huge fallen tree trunk for the night. I watched in awe as the creatures above us created the shadow of a dance which reflected on the ground we walked upon squelching beneath our feet. My eyes drifted to watch in disbelief as Hedwinn morphed around the site, he was so fast that my eyes were barely able to follow him.

He grinned showing off his perfectly white teeth for a second before he continued to set up. I couldn't believe what I had seen or rather what I had caught a glimpses of. The bark of the tree beneath me was tediously uncomfortable, I folded up my jacket and wedged it between the bark and the muck on my jeans.

Looking up I realised that in just a few seconds Hedwinn had created every campers dream, in the time it took me to make myself comfortable he had cleared away an entire 10 foot radius of every fallen branch, twig and leaf. My eyes followed various deadly trigger wires which he had planted around us, each one was so sinisterly and meticulously placed. If you took a heavy breath beside them then you would surely meet a bitter end. I shuddered - thank the lord I wasn't a sleep walker. I had no idea exactly what those wires would trigger and I had no desire to find out, eventually he took a much deserved seat beside me.

"How the hell did you do that?" I stared at him impatient for a response.

"Practice." I laughed. The purple sleeping bag he pulled out for me was rather brilliantly my favourite colour, absolutely nothing was out of its place or in any way obtrusive. Hedwinn had done his finest work to make the best of this poor situation, he meticulously hung twilight decorations reminiscent of candles above us. Each tiny light was skilfully wrapped around the nearby tree trunks fuelled by his touch, it lit up the camp site like a haunted Christmas tree it was unexplainably beautiful and strangely hypnotic as they twinkled.

I smiled as the fire he constructed blazed, as I unzipped my backpack rummaging through it I found my mobile. Holding it up to the animated sky in hope of attracting a signal but I had no luck, deflated I placed it back into the side compartment. I turned my attention back to Hedwinn with whom I didn't have to ask too many questions for him to open up and answer my queries one by one.

It felt like I was reciting questions I had already asked a million times just not out loud and not with any hope of ever getting a response. I kept my fingers crossed for something, anything, and everything.

"Our world is not something you would ever stumble across on any mortal website, nor is it something that would be spoke about through the lips of beings less significant then you or I. Avalon is host to hundreds of vampires lead by 3 leaders, myself being one of them. I belong to the Triquils, every millennium or so a vampire is headhunted to govern Avalon and its leaders, he or she is usually an acting leader of a coven. I was chosen thirty years ago to protect Avalon and its people. The 3 main covens, Triquils, Gohinease and Phelium have the greatest following of vampires. But some remain rouge.

"This arrangement for me to guide you is by no means accidental, it's all part of a higher collective purpose if we allow ourselves to integrate into what you would see as a normal society. We would certainly not be honouring the codes and sacrifices which our elders lived and died for if we overstep the boundaries.

"My great grandfather and creator of Avalon, Rayabis and his mate Aluma set our way of life many moons ago. We all found out the difficult way, just what can happen when Uppers discover our kind."

"Uppers?" He nodded as my mind scrambled over the influx information he was feeding me.

"Those who exist on the world above us, the world you were brought into."

"Oh so, what happened, when they found out?" I swallowed, feeling the tension in the air swirl around us like a hurricane taking with it my anxiety and replacing it with confidence and curiosity. "If I told you that then Raybis' work to ensure you all forgot would be in vain."

My eyes popped open. "What do you mean? He wiped out the entire world's memory's? You can do that?"

I was astonished, coughing up the sweet hot liquid I was coaxing in my hands barely able to hear his warm charismatic laugh. I was beginning to see this man so differently, Hedwinn is young, early to mid-thirties at least, I smiled as I caught my breath back.

"Well?" His smile grew as he spoke.

"Luckily that wasn't necessary that would have surely brought him to his knees, just the west coast."

What? "Can you just, wipe people's memories like that?"

"We restarted the day, the way it was supposed to occur, *normal* and grey." He shuddered.

"Time zones are a funny thing." He gestured to my cup. "Drink your half-mast before it becomes cold and sour." I repeated his words back to him

"Half-mast?"

"Yes, but before I tell you the ingredients, do you like it?" I nodded, resentment at the starting blocks. "It's sanguinello, with a hint of blood." I instantly dropped the white polystyrene cup. "Blood?" I remained motionless as I eagerly awaited his response.

"Donated, we have an Upper source, he works in a clinic - it's the discarded blood of mammals."

I coughed, again. "By mammals, you mean, humans?"

He smiled. "We never kill Uppers Eva, we only use the smallest of quantities possible, to keep us going, otherwise..." He shook his head as my stomach churned.

"This contact of yours, who is he or she?"

"He is employed at a top clinic where they process donations, some of which is contaminated with diseases and pesticides, completely unsuitable to Uppers. However, as we remain immune to such illnesses. We can make valuable use of the generous donation." I smiled slightly with sickly relief, still in shock at the liquid I had consumed.

As I looked down at the puddle of half-mast I couldn't help but think of the parasites swarming within it. Cancer took the life of my uncle, diseases take lives every day, HIV, Plasma Cell Disorders. I suddenly felt the still hot liquid shoot back up my throat, moving my head to the side I threw up uncontrollably. Tears streaming down my cheeks as a shell shocked Hedwinn patted my back, not speaking.

Completely humiliated I grabbed my bag and took out a cotton towel, scrubbing my face.

"Are you alright?" I heard a bewildered Hedwinn ask.

I nodded and swirling the last of my cranberry juice in my mouth before spitting it out. I took a seat on the all too comfortable blown up bed courtesy of my new friend complete with covers and even enough space left over so that I could place my phone and a clean set of clothes in beside me in preparation for tomorrow.

I pulled the covers up around my shoulders just watching Hedwinn as he spoke to me.

"There is one more immortal that I must inform or rather warn you of his name is Magnus, he is or rather *was* 4th in line to take my place as head of Avalon, however he doesn't possess the same kindness as the rest of those who you will become acquainted with. He will pull every trick, cut every corner to get ahead, please take this warning seriously Eva. I cannot promise your paths will not cross in the future but a halfblooded creature such as you, in already heightened authority-"

He didn't finish the sentence but the words he spoke sent shivers shooting down my spine, I could do nothing but nod wearily in response.

I laid my head down once a beautifully calm silence had broken out. I knew from the words that I was just told - tonight sleep would be an improbable blessing. In the forefront of my mind I knew that if I allowed myself to give into sleep, I'd wake up back in one of the two prisons I had been trapped in recently. Either the one with my too perfect sister Amelia alongside my intolerably blind mother, to whom I couldn't do anything right for always being in the wrong, and of course the deadly trap Julia kept me in.

I couldn't let myself give up on this chance at a new and all together better life.

So, I didn't sleep that night instead I listened to the howl of the trees, the echo of woodpeckers in the distance and the continuous sound of dead branches toppling over one another several miles away. I couldn't help but repeatedly check my phone, praying I could get a signal before the battery died.

The only sound which I didn't find myself tuning into was Hedwinn he left about an hour after I set my head down with a promise he would return.

I rose from my cocoon the second the sun presented itself on the horizon; Beatles and ants surrounded me and to my disbelieve I could hear their tiny insignificant movements. They scurried together at such a speed the sound from them was a soft tuneful hum. Each one of them feeding on the half-mast I had accidently dropped to the floor last night. I shuddered as the creatures had surrounded my sleeping bag, I jumped to my feet from beneath the covers whilst trying to shake them from my hair and slapping my legs to get them off me, shuddering as I stepped away from the riddled sleeping bag.

Not exactly the best way to start the day, however the bright sun had just began to beam a bright light between the woven tree tops. I climbed up the tallest tree to watch the mesmerising display, as I studied the magnificent blinding mornings sun sounding natures silent alarm waking all the birds nesting up in the trees, it was the day's first flutter of life.

Who needs an automated alarm clock when every morning I could wake up to this - an untouched spectacular habitat, it was so beautiful. I watched with fascination but I was pulled out of it by the sudden reappearance of Hedwinn, had he been gone all night?

I abruptly leaped down from the treetop landing effortlessly behind him unthinkingly I tapped him on the shoulder, in the same instant he grabbed my wrist and flung me across the site like a featherweight rag doll. I landed against the stump of a tree, the lights from the nights campfire tumbled down over my shoulders and down by my side. The moment my body slammed against the truck of the tree, the sound of a roaring crunch spread through the forest like a lightning bolt. My body slumping, and for a few seconds I prayed the sound wasn't my spine crunching to smithereens, I moved my legs with anxious success.

At the very least I wasn't paralysed, but my body had not gotten away unharmed it took me a second to place myself. I continued groaning as my eyes focused on his face and the bandage he was already wrapping around my wrist. I shook my head as he apologised profusely.

"Evangeline, I didn't know it was you! It was instinct, I can't apologise enough."

I forced a smile in a foolish attempt to mask the pain which was coursing from the top of my head down to the base of my spine, and to the tips of my fingers. To help minimise his guilt I stumbled to my feet rubbing my hands on the sides of my jeans, holding back a groan as my left wrist snapped back into place.

I turned around to see the tree had fallen, it gave way exactly in half from the force he had thrown me, the sound must have been from the tree as it took the full force. I ran my fingers through my long messy hair, surprised over the lack of blood around the main impact point I smiled with relief.

He kept fiddling with my wrist as I flexed my fingers, looking into his eyes to give a reassuring smile.

"I'm fine, it was an honest mistake we should get going right?" He nodded with a heavy sigh of liberation.

I gathered together my minimalistic few things after Hedwinn had built me a makeshift changing room. Luckily I was able to change in a matter of seconds. In my head I only counted to 4 before I was out of my pyjamas and into my new set of clothes - something of a record I would imagine. The buttons on my jeans, the hook of my bra, and the hem of my top all straightened out.

With my bag now over my shoulder, I watched Hedwinn disassemble the camping equipment managing to condense the items into a bag which was only a few centimetres bigger than mine. The man was certainly an odd but experienced character; he wore a long grey robe tied at the centre over a black buttoned shirt, his skin was pale white, his eyes a piercing black for a majority of the time. Apart from conversations relating to his family and sustenance Hedwinn's eyes as we know, reacted rather remarkably.

They would change colour as if they were pixelated or something, constantly changing I had found myself transfixed by them on several occasions. Having to remind myself to stop looking and start listening.

His shoes resembled the Ted Baker boots my father used to wear to work although Hedwinn's were meticulously clean and missing the trademark logo. I laughed at the prospect of him going into a high street store to purchase the latest seasons trends. His chestnut brown hair was parted perfectly in the centre which only made his eyes bloom a more prominent shadow of black.

I had noticed Hedwinn didn't wear cologne, hair jell, aftershave but somehow he smelt incredible, like crushed wild berries and squashed grapes. It was certainly an odd odour for a man but I was becoming familiar with it.

We headed off again, this time in a north easterly direction Hedwinn took the lead and he remained irritating secretive about our destination. Recharging my nervousness; we stopped just before noon to eat as our stomachs roared with hunger. I observed with curiosity as

Hedwinn knelt into the long grass, it was there that he picked up a clucking brown chicken nestled in the dead auburn undergrowth.

"The rules state we may only feed from an Uppers' animal carcass once the creature falls victim to natural causes." I hadn't noticed the sudden silence of the previously squawking chicken.

"Sometimes, old age can be a dear friend and since you have not yet discovered your own dietary needs as a member of our kind, this will have to suffice."

He said with a confident silk to his tone he knew how to make his words difficult to argue against - not that I wanted to argue. I was practically salivating at the prospect of finally having something substantial to eat, I couldn't remember the last time I had tasted something so mouth-wateringly satisfying.

"Thank you, I didn't particularly enjoy the barbaric killing for sustenance that I endured under Julia."

His head snapped up from examining the animal to me in an instant, I could hear the crack in his neck jerking with his sudden movement.

"Is she still alive?" His previously relaxed manner suddenly transformed to a stiff uncomfortable stance, it was at this moment I noticed there were so many different sides to Hedwinn. His calm and collected side, his boyish laughing side and now I was being introduced to his cautious and practically paranoid side. I missed laughing Hedwinn, as I spoke, his troubled expression did not waver.

"Well, yes, she captured me and my half-sister Amelia a few weeks ago, that is how I became to be half vampire." He nodded slowly; I was a little offended by his lack of knowledge on how I came to be here, which provoked me to doubt his intellect in other equally controversial areas and it also triggered me to ask more penetrative questions. He was keeping once again quiet regards to how he knew my location in the first place, he continued to query about my experience with the murderous Julia.

He seemed completely oblivious to just how uncomfortable I was talking about it, he wouldn't let the agonizing topic drop.

"I see, it's impressive that you exist to tell the tale, not many can say that. Julia is Magnus' daughter; fortunately she inherited his fine hospitality and their combined impeccable traits are renowned."

I laughed softly at his sarcastic remarks and then reflected over the sinister underlining meaning of his ominous words. "So, how come you didn't know she was still around?" I looked to him as he began plucking and cooking chicken over a selection of burning tree branches he had been gathering along route, which made me feel stupid for wondering why he was collecting them in bundles on route.

"She and her father, the man I warned you about went rogue around 3 months ago. The coven hasn't had any contact from them since then, we always assumed the worst.

"It's very rare for any member of our kind to make it outside the compound, but then again they're not exactly a *usual* pair that you can apply common statistics too." I nodded, thinking back to my lone wondering and what it would have lead too if Hedwinn hadn't of found me when he did.

I began to devour the chicken Hedwinn had prepared as the sun beamed though the bare branches of the trees, the light caused the mark on my arm to ache; I rubbed the area over my open buttoned cardigan in an attempt to soothe the pain which was intensifying at an excruciating rate.

Luckily we were finished quickly which allowed us to move onto denser territories with a cooler spring breeze circling the air as each hour flew by. I struggled my way up what I was promised to be the last of a million hills we had climbed to reach our destination. Once we made it to the top I took a generously long moment to admire the overwhelming sea of red, stretching as far as the eye could see. Until the obscure figure of a man caught my attention as he walked towards the centre of the poppy field, leaving a trail behind him which we could later follow.

I watched as Hedwinn and the man exchanged a nod as we began our decent though the red painted fields to meet the stranger who was dressed similarly to Hedwinn, except he wore an additional hat which shaded half of his face. He conversed with a clear but unfamiliar British accent, which was both intoxicating and endearing. As he and Hedwinn spoke, I speculated if where we were going was filled with equally charming characters, to make me feel even more painstakingly average. I had just gotten away from Amelia, my 'oh so' perfect sister whose shadow had become my undesirable home with expectations I couldn't adhere to.

"We still haven't heard anything regarding Julia and Magnus." He stated whilst glancing to me between myself and Hedwinn with each word    I suddenly felt overwhelmed with self-consciousness as he stared. I wish I had some sort of indication as to what these people were expecting from me - as a newcomer, as a friend of Hedwinn's and even more worryingly, as an escapee of Julia's.

I wanted so badly to fit their ideals, I just wish I knew the exact specifications required I likened it to riding a bike for the first time without stabilisers, thrilling but dangerous. Of course the worst case scenario there was a badly scrapped knee, the worst probability here didn't bare a second thought. "I have an update; I'll get you up to speed on the way." Hedwinn replied in an assertive tone that he was yet to direct toward me, I arched my brow as the man held out his hand to meet mine.

"And you must be Evangeline, I am Verdon ma'am."

He bowed swooping one arm behind his back; I pursed my ruby lips together for a second to stop the laughter which was building in my throat ready to burst out, finally bringing composure back to my face.

"Call me Eva, it's a pleasure to meet you Verdon but, you do not need to bow."

I smiled gracefully as I shook his hand, I was made increasingly aware of Hedwinn's eyes over us both. While Hedwinn was twice my elder I felt a great deal of safety with him around. He had gained my trust which given recent events was not an easy feat. I stuck to his side as Verdon led the way through the field and it didn't take long for us to be submerged under the branches of another forest. Beneath the moonlight I noticed that Verdon possessed a similar pendant to mine and here I was thinking that the pendant was one of a kind.

The pendant that hung around Verdon's neck grew a brighter and brighter shade of green, till it was luminous. It was shaped like a raindrop, a really large raindrop with carved edges and had a fine point at the tip. I placed my hand to my neck, running my fingers along the sharp outline of my pendant however it soon lost my attention as my feet grew sluggish after thirty hours of constant walking. It was difficult to keep myself motivated when I had absolutely no idea on how much longer we would have to walk, or what we were walking towards.

At long last we made it to a humongous Circus tree, I was amazed at the sight of the bark it was the exact epitome of nature's exquisite handiwork beaded so perfectly as if it had been stitched beneath a microscope. I had never seen anything like it. I had been taught about trees in my rigorous science classes at college but they stressed the rarity of this particular tree. Sun light streamed through the hollow shaped hearts and ringlets between the bark. I ran my hand along the smooth braised bark whilst biting my lower lip, although I was stunned I must admit to say I was slightly annoyed that we had travelled miles upon miles in search of a tree, would be an understatement.

I hastily stepped aside as Verdon grabbed the wrists of Hedwinn and I but before I could pull myself free in a single blink my feet were no longer beneath me. My vision was obstructed by an extraordinarily blinding green light. So bright it was almost burning my eyes, I sharply closed my heavy lids again, squeezing them together as tight as I could. The light was more powerful than I expected, I couldn't block it out.

I no longer felt Verdon's grip over my wrist as I placed my hands over my eyes; my body was a mangled uncontrollable mess as I continued helplessly falling. A strong relentless wind galled and howled relentlessly past me. It was as though I'd fallen down into a huge manhole. One moment I was stood beside the stunning tree - the next my back was against the floor. Had the ground actually gobbled me up...?

My manhole theory was becoming increasingly unlikely - it certainly didn't smell as you would expect. I couldn't sense anything at all until a few tweeting birds had my eyes open instantaneously with amazing choral tones never previously heard on my ears. Slowly parting my fingers, it took a long moment for them to focus on the perky bright clear blue sky.

# 3. WELCOME TO AVALON

I could feel my body's sore limbs against the cold marble floor but I didn't dare move, what have I gotten myself into?

After a few moments of silence I felt it was safe enough to finally attempt getting up. As I stumbled to my feet I regained my balance but my eyes still struggled to focus after the previous assault of light, blinking repeated I held myself up against the tree.

As I gained my balance, to my amazement I was still in the presence of the tree. The soles of my trainers had begun leaving prints of dirt against a stunning marble floor. Leaning over I unlaced my shoes, slipping them off, the cold floor began penetrating my socks. With my eyes now adjusted I began exploring my new surroundings.

Had I fallen victim to another hallucination? I couldn't tell.

Once I had regained my balance and vision I clambered around the room; I rolled my shoulders back and forth then rubbed my face with my hands - no wounds. As soon as I was positive I wasn't under the influence of a striking delusion, I proceeded to peek and tread around the deliriously beautiful spell binding room. Miraculously the strong roots of the circus tree had weeded deep into the marble floor. As I lifted my head up I was overwhelmed by my surroundings on the bright white walls, stunning hand painted family portraits displayed in gleaming bronze edged decorative frames.

Each individual was dressed to impress; polished pendants, luxuriously beautiful, smiling, proud faces - I was far too apprehensive to touch anything. I was so accident prone, I shouldn't be allowed to be anywhere near these irreplaceable artefacts. My mouth hung open as I noticed every stunning individual in the paintings wore the same pendant as I. Suddenly I felt the heavy weight of it as I walked toward the walls partition. Hovering my finger over the lettering beneath each of the priceless picture frames, each one reading unfamiliar names. Ysan, Timbers, Blacket and finally I ran my finger over the last name Carter.

I studied the pictures with bewilderment and admiration until I was unexpectedly interrupted, the sound of heavy foot steps behind me; I looked over my shoulder my long messy hair shielding half of my face, peering through the binding bark of the tree towards a gigantic black door. I bit down so hard on my lip that it began to bleed, the large door slowly opened; my heart was thumping uncontrollably for those few manic seconds.

Thankfully my fear was put to rest as I was welcomed by Hedwinn's familiar friendly face.

"My apologies Eva, I had to quickly run out to warn the others of your imminent arrival. I hope you will not hold my negligence against me." Others, how many others? I gulped. He looked at me with an expression that I had become very familiar with over the past few days. His apologetic eyes so optimistic in contrast to the jet black glossy paint of the door, covering the door and its frame which he was stood beside. As Hedwinn closed the door behind him I couldn't help but notice he wasn't wearing a wedding ring, I respected him enough not to query his marital status.

It seems incredibly odd to me that Hedwinn would be single at all, he's handsome, annoyingly well-educated and very level headed. Maybe the rules of attraction were different here. Hedwinn had stressed their disliking to material possessions, maybe that applies to wedding rings and jewellery alike. Accept of course our pendants which I found were more practical than sentimental or ornamental for that matter.

His apology was sweet as ever. "Of course not, it gave me a chance to admire these stunning paintings, they are so incredibly beautiful, but I have to ask how the hell did we get here and where is Verdon?"

Right now, I didn't need another wordy explanation I just needed something I could understand amongst all this madness.

My body language pointing out the ridiculousness and almost hilarity of our location, so far removed from the fields we had just been wondering through for the past few days. I frowned as he treaded towards me with a smile; he began patting the tree as he spoke with loud ambitious pride.

"This is one of twelve; very rich portals providing a bridge between this world and the one you know. Verdon is the transporter - you can think of him as our covens messenger. I thought if I told you about the landing you would be reluctant to come with us."

Whilst laughing off my superficial wound I spoke. "Someone should put a mattress down there or something." Whilst laughing off my superficial wounds,

He too admired the paintings, stood shoulder to shoulder.

This world was so obviously different to the one I knew. Right down to the air that circulated around every room. It was so much cleaner mainly because of the astounding roofless room which also welcomed in the ever bright sun. I was overcome with an irrational sense of belonging as if this was my world. With the Triquil members I felt at home, Avalon was certainly a wonderful refuge. I felt increasingly foolish for my previous internal slander of Hedwinn's mental state when we first met, I grinned to myself at my prior epic misjudgement.

Hedwinn and I walked side by side through the grand hall; it become abundantly obvious the portraits all had one thing in common, serene beauty. Although one woman who sat alone amongst the other group portraits grabbed my attention. Her slender hands tied prominently behind her back. Her ankles were tightly strapped to the chair legs using a combination of leather and steel chains, her eyes were a devastating manifestation of a deranged psychosis. Hedwinn noticed my attraction to the image, but there was a long pause before he spoke.

"I see you've come across Luciana her unusually brilliant talent led to her incarceration and inevitable self-destruction." I frowned at the thought of a woman who was once constricted by something that was supposed to be her gift - she looked absolutely terrified. And in the presence of her stare, I was also equally terrified.

"What happened to her?" I couldn't keep my eyes off the strange woman - the pain in her black eyes scorning me like a great lightning bolt striking through my chest and to my soul. Observing at the woman's portrait was equal to looking into the eyes of a horrifying ghostly phantom.

"Luciana was a once very gifted woman, she possessed the astonishing ability to familiarise herself with an individual and develop the ability see through their eyes.

"For example she could have thought of our missing members Julia and Magnus and she could peer through their eyes without permission. She could also listen into conversations which could unlock the key to their location and potential forthcoming motivations."

Hedwinn looked down to me with an arched brow as I spoke my next question. "That's incredible, what led to this?" I gestured back to the portrait which didn't exactly match his description of a woman with a remarkable amount of supremacy at her fingertips.

"Over time she began to lose control over whose life she could peer into, nor could she control the durations of her visions or even control the duration in which she was able to see. In the end she lost sight of her own identity and her ability ruled her life, for years she valiantly fought against it, but she became the barer of many strangers' secrets. It drove her to eventually take her own life.

"We maintain this portrait to remind us not to lose sight of who we are amongst the wonders of this life which has been given to us. She certainly places things into a very perspective frame for us all wouldn't you agree?"

For the first time I was speechless - it was devastating to even think of a woman so completely vulnerable to the life she was handed. It lead her to a place at which she had no other way out then to end her own life it was horrifying. I think Hedwinn was a little bit taken aback by my lack of response to his unforgettable words; he placed his hand to my shoulder and glanced down to me.

"She is a rare case; her problems stemmed far greater than just difficulties with her talent." I nodded once again, my tongue continued to play disobedience rendering me speechless, before I allowed the tale to sink into my skin.

I continued walking beside the portrayed wall, until finally Hedwinn directed me from the grand hall. It had undoubtedly left a grave impression on my first visit. Just before leaving I took one last look around to absorb its grandeur.

As I followed Hedwinn we headed down a hallway which was filled with more and more paintings, we walked passed additional closed doors baring names engraved into gold lettered plates. I was continually amazed by the lack of roof over head, it was constant throughout the entire building.

The more I thought about it, it seemed almost illogical to hide such a beautiful blue cloudless sky, it was more beautiful than any amount of decoration, created by man or vampire.

At last we reached a door with my name 'Carter' on a gold plate nailed into the drown varnished door, an eager Hedwinn nodded me forward. I tightly gripped the round golden door handle I slowly opened the door to a cloudy overcast chamber decorated with my favourite colour; purple. As I took a few cautious steps forward I noticed an abundance of lilac tulips delicately placed above the patterned purple and grey covers of the king sized bed. It was huge, clearly far too much room for just me. As I thought about how much the excess space would make me miss him further, to my astonishment the oak structured bed began to shrink before my eyes, my mouth falling open.

A vine of long stemmed flowers covered the enchanted frame of the bed, Hedwinn followed me inside, I watched as he tapped his chin inspecting the rapid evolution.

"How very interesting." His voice took my attention away from appreciating the lifelike room, with an apparent life and personality of its own.

"What, do you mean?" I replied with curiosity. "This is your room, from the moment you touched the brass handle, this space it adapted to become everything you desire in an area of boundless magnitude. A combination of emotional reflections and general necessities, you must be having troubled thoughts dear." I felt the cold droplets of rain trickle down my cheek as I detected a picture of myself and Tyler. It stood proudly on a small wooden cabinet beneath the stream of growing flowers. I slumped down on the bed as I took the picture between my two hands, the silver hallmarked frame held the picture so beautifully. I traced my fingertips over Tyler's face, a tear ran down my cheek. I watched it fall in the refection of the glass which protected the image.

Over the past few days, in the company of Hedwinn, I became so completely transfixed in this new world. I had completely lost sight of my previous mundane reality, in just a few short hours. I felt my once rapid heart bleed beneath my ribs as every beat was more agonising then the last, I heard an obviously uncomfortable Hedwinn leave my room. I can only assume that he didn't know how to comfort me which I understood. I woozily laid my head on the pillow as the light in the room dimmed to nothing greater than a shadow. Due to the thick formation of rain clouds gathering overhead, cold; I clung to the photograph fearing it would disappear in my arms along with everything else.

I mourned for Tyler, hiding beneath the drenched bed covers as this part of the building rapidly became my own personalised hell. The thunderstorm kept me awake hour after hour, lightning bolts darting down within inches of the shaken bed.

I assumed the fettle position, hugging my knees, the photo pressing against my chest as I breathed bleakly. I kept waking restlessly throughout the long night until eventually I sat up grabbing a pen, and piece of paper from the newly resurrected drawers beside my bed, finally my room had produced something non-life threatening.

I consciously rolled the red pen back and forth in my hand between my thumb and index finger, consciously chewing on my lip as my head fought with my heart over the appropriate words to write on the paper. I couldn't pull together the correct sentences, I didn't even know if he would want to hear everything I needed to say. I couldn't imagine him hating me so much that he would tear up the letter, regardless of the content. But what if he did? More so, what if he didn't...?

I began it with two words that I have been so desperate to tell him since the moment we said goodbye. I knew I couldn't come back, I didn't even know how to get back, or if I was being honest with myself, I didn't even know if I wanted to ever go back. I was more of a burden to him then I was a girlfriend, I now had a place with my name carved into the door - I now have a home. A potentially new family and a theoretically greater purpose. Finally I wrote:

I'm sorry.

I knew these words may fall upon his uninterested and already hurt ears. So I wrote them again and again to ensure they were emphasised and not underestimated.

I'm sorry.
I'm sorry.
I'm sorry.

Tyler, I'm not writing this letter in the hope that you will forgive me for the decision I'm faced with. I don't warrant your forgiveness, I'm just writing to tell you that I'm alright. Not in a ditch or holding a spot on a street corner. I'm safe so you can call off the search party! I do miss you, I miss you so much.
Every day I carry you in my heart and, it's not by choice. I must be going crazy because I still feel your presence around me in all that I see and do. I would tell you what I have stumbled upon, but I doubt you would believe me if I did. I just wish you could see it.
I close my eyes and I can see you, I fall asleep and I dream of you. I can still catch your scent occasionally flowing through the air and I turn to see if you are near, even though I know that would be impossible.
But I cannot deny who I am, no more than I can deny that I love you. I hope that you will at least, in time, understand this decision. I love you, Tyler. Please never doubt that.

I love you Tyler, please never doubt that.
Your Eva.

x

I wrote the name and address as neatly as I could, in order to ensure it would be delivered to the correct place. I slipped on my shoes and quietly closed my bedroom door behind me, leaving my miserable room.

I walked back to the tree which had brought me here, if the tree could bring me here then it could certainly send things back, couldn't it? I slid the letter into the trunk of the tree and watched it slowly evaporate, a few speckles of ink were the last fragments to disappear. Turning around, I took in a hefty gasp as I was met by an unfamiliar but majestically porcelain face.

A woman, the first I had encountered since arriving here. She had short ringlet blond hair which framed her heart shaped face; she wore a long golden dress which made me feel immediately out of place, I however was stood opposite wearing my converses shoes, skinny jeans and Tyler's old navy jumper. I watched as her bright marvellous eyes almost scowling down on me, I nervously retracted my hands from the inside of the sleeves of my pullover.

She is truly stunning. "Eva love, it's wonderful to finally meet you, but you must get dressed for the big meet and greet this evening. You can't very well meet the rest of the coven dressed like that, now can you?" Meet and greet? I clenched my teeth together.

She smiled and walked me to her room through the corridors of empire. The sound of her heels echoed around the walls of the beautiful halls.

"I don't have any other 'dress' appropriate clothes." I confessed with an awkward belligerent smile.

She looked at me with an amused almost ecstatic grin.

"Oh don't worry about it. Kayleigh is a great seamstress and I myself have some skill when it comes to a pencil and a sketch pad, what are you? An 8?"

I nodded sheepishly, I knew what was coming next, I could see the excitement in her eyes, I groaned. Whilst some girls and women at my age would leap at the chance of having a fitted dress by a woman who clearly was familiar with style, I on the other hand was less than enthusiastic. I glanced at the tree again over my shoulder, giving one last thought to the letter I sent before I was led towards her room.

The gold slate on her door read Genevieve and Kayleigh Avalon, as I followed the woman inside suddenly I was overwhelmed by the scents of burning oils and lavender. My eyes widened as I set sight upon a woman who looked exactly like Genevieve, emerging from the en suite at the far side of the room. Twins, I smiled to myself.

I presumed from what I had been told, there is typically an evil and a pleasant one; at this point I was certain I had met the pleasant one. I waited apprehensively to see if that was indeed the case or just an old wives tale. It took me by surprise when Kayleigh the second sister strutted over to me wearing a plunged navy blue knee length dress, with an inviting smile upon her glossed rosy lips. She shook my hand with excitement and interest, I flexed my fingers after we shook, to see if I could still feel them. I laughed softly as my hand quickly recovered.

I hooked my tingling thumbs into the belt catches on my dark blue faded jeans, throwing my nervous habit into overdrive as Kayleigh ran a tape measure over me. I took this opportunity to familiarise myself with the room. The walls were painted a strong peach which reflected the blinding sun, beaming in overhead and through the triple glazed glass windows at either side. If this gave any indication of their personalities, it was certainly a reflection I should surround myself with.

If the state of my room was anything to go by, I could use positive 'glass half full' role models. My last positive ray of sunshine was no longer mine, I was lost without that someone who I had always depended upon to raise my spirits.

I couldn't exactly complain as the decisions were on my part, this loss was an uncomfortable compromise. My brow rose as I inhaled the scent of camomile pulling me from my thoughts. I watched as Genevieve strut over to me holding a pale yellow mug of tea, complete with saucer, spoon and a small cube of sugar, I smiled but she looked at me with concern.

"You have so much on your shoulders for such a young spirit,. I I remember correctly, these small supplements are known to help calm your nervous." I smiled at her words with countless gratitude. "Thank you Genevieve." As she handed me the mug of tea my eyes were drawn to a black bruise on her upper arm, it stood out so readily against her pale skin. Within seconds Kayleigh noticed my interest and cleared her throat to divert my attention. I took a sip of the sweet tea.

"This tea is really good." I attempted to hold back my curiosity but I couldn't prevent my mouth from forming the words that I would later regret letting slip.

"I don't mean to pry Genevieve but is that a birth mark?"

She snorted in response to my inquisitive ill-informed inquiry about the penetrating black scar.

"Eva, Avalon hasn't always been the 'safe haven' you see today. Magnus is not a forgiving or remotely rational individual to say the very least, no this is a mark of punishment." The twins had a habit of using their hands a lot whilst talking, as if they were controlling puppets. Their hands wavered constantly; slowly I lifted my free hand till it was near the battle scar.

"May I?" The sisters both looked simultaneously to one another and then back to me with weary expressions, followed by a simultaneous nod. I bit my lip as I ran my fingertip over the bruise, it certainly felt like nothing greater than a birth mark to me, not sore or tender; I concentrated all of my energy on the marking. Instinct is a powerful and uncontrollable force, my soul or what was left of it told me not to stop.

A few seconds later I watched as small bolts of electricity zapping her bruise, the source of which was my very own fingertips. The broken skin shrunk inch by inch; it was as if I was removing an age old ink stain from her skin, lighting up each molecule. My fingers became numb as I took away every single partial of pain that she was baring. I pulled my hand away as I observed her revitalised pale skin I stepped back as the humanitarian in me rationalised the situation, I accidentally dropped the cup of tea and all its accompaniments. I jumped instinctively hearing it smash, fragments of the cup were now scattered along the previously immaculately clean white floor. I grimaced as I felt an agonising jolt of pain grabbing at my arm, I hesitantly turned my back to the girls, lifting up my sleeve slightly I gasped to see that the scar had been transferred onto my now friable skin.

"Are you alright?" Quizzed Kayleigh, her hands gesturing to and fro waiting for my response, probably counting the anxious breaths which sprung from my lips. I was careful as my expression showed in the mirror positioned directly opposite as my frown subsided. I relaxed my cheek bones and turned back towards them both, forcing a smile.

"I'll live." As quickly as opportunity allowed I found my way back to my room, that night I sat up examining my mark and contemplating the stability of my inherently bruised skin.

I thought about the last time I injured myself, my clumsiness playing havoc. I was at my grandmother's; I will always remember her reaction. If she were here now she would have gotten out her tin of multi-coloured plasters from the cabinet beside the radio.

I went on to remember the evenings I spent at my quaint grandmother's house, I would watch her sleep in the dingy chair for endless hours. It was so easy to lose myself into these thoughts. I lay back with my head resting against the pillow and watched the animation play overhead, my own thoughts presented above me, the sky replaced with images of my grandmother and I.

I reminisced nonstop, enjoying the comfort of memories I hadn't forgotten. She would fall asleep and when she did I would immediately turn down the thermostat a few notches, as well as the volume on the old TV set. She always had it so loud; she never did take advantage of the hearing aid she had enquired long before I was born.

Personally I think she just regarded the figures on the small screen as a form of company. And now the images of her were accompanying me on my first night.

The walls in my grandmother's house was decorated with a collage of the pictures from my childhood, along with her own, my mother's and Amelia's. Although I distinctly remember there being a lack of reminiscent stories about my grandfather.

Generally my only memory of him is how he would always smell of tobacco, although he never smoked from his pipe in front of us, and he took care of my grandmother. She was a woman of few demands, she always made sure that everyone who visited her left with a full stomach and a confidence like no other. As I recalled the confidence she had preached to me, about always being yourself, fighting for what you believe in. Lessons I needed to remember now above all other times.

I had to be honest with myself, what is the worst thing that could happen if I told them about what I discovered today?

Exploitation didn't seem to be their objective with me and if it was, they were so far failing. The twins and Hedwinn had gone out of their way to ensure my comfort - everything here is perfect. Blissfully and unequivocally perfect. I was waiting for my Truman boat to hit the wall.

Without a doubt the most spellbinding and utterly outrageous room within the humble kingdom of Avalon had caught my eye after I had once again forgotten my route back to my bedroom from the dining area. Even though I had lost the feeling of hunger and humility, I was certainly enjoying the company of the entire coven, with them I felt a heart-warming sense of freedom. I'm amazed Hedwinn hasn't noticed my navigational incompetence yet, I bet he hasn't even thought of putting up signs or at least providing me with a map. My curiosity provoked my next step as I spotted the entrance to a mesmerising room I was yet to explore, the size of Avalon never seized to astonish me.

The entrance to the room was a very decorative archway formed with worn stone, guarding the way toward very steep steps beyond. My flat shoes clapped down against the cracking marble slabs as I stepped down them one by one. I glanced around the curved corner toward a lengthy room, before I reached the rustic door I was met with a thick sheet of insect-riddled, spiders web. The web flowed between the walls like a filthy cloth. As I squirmed my way through it, I couldn't help but grow more and more inquisitive of the residents living behind the now visible entrance.

The wooden door swung open and the smell of rodents hit me instantly, I covered my sensitive nose with the back of my hand. To my relief the room didn't contain the troll-like person I was expecting. Instead the only resident was an enormous lifelike statue more than twice my height. As I admired the manikin I imagined the hours, days or even months it must have taken the artists sculpting every inch of the beings lifelike features.

My eyes marvelled at his stone carved waistcoat, the line of pristine buttons, the incredible detail of his aged hands and his long pianist fingers. The sculpture was a piece of art an aesthetic labour of love, everything was undeniably exquisite right down to the sculptures ornamental shoe laces which had been tied to perfection.

Leaning up onto the very tips of my toes I was barely able to run my fingers along the crease on the statues chin. Jumping backward as a gust of air brushed past my unpainted fingertips, in stepping back I was able to see the beings face more clearly. The thin stone eyelashes clashing together colliding to the sound of my heart, overcome with a combination of shock and utter astonishment. I clutched onto my pale nightdress as to my amazement, the enormous statue parted its grey creased lips and began to speak.

"My, oh my young lady." His frightfully deep voice made the hairs along my pale arms stand up and the echo of his voice shook my bones. I was unable to produce a response I kept my quavering lips pressed together. As I continued inspecting the glorious male figurine, slowly he lifted his right leg placing it wearily in front of the left, I also took another step backwards as rubble from the wall he was leaning against fell to my bare icy feet. When his he finally stepped forward, he cracked his neck from side to side. The sound was bone crushing and terrifying, and with it a flinch shook my cold body. I lifted my hand to rest on his chest as I feared he could collapse within an instant, then we would both be history. Once he was finally stable, apprehensively I let go.

"Young lady, never have I been startled to such a degree." As he scolded me for a moment I regretted denying the earlier requests to walk me back to my room, from Hedwinn and the others. If only I wasn't so stubborn, beside them, I never would have become lost, my thoughts were interrupted. "On the contrary I am happy to be startled by an old friend."

I watched with a bemused smile, his large arm which was easily the size of my entire body extended towards me leisurely. "Mr Cornelius Avalon Jackson at your service."

I reached out my hand to hold his, as we shook the rough texture of his hand scraped repeatedly against my skin; I tried not to wince as his fingers felt like sandpaper against the back of my knuckles.

I frowned as I thought about his words 'an old friend.' I wasn't old, and to my knowledge I certainly wasn't a friend of his. I thought I better clear the murky air and formally introduce myself.

"I'm Ev-" Before I could finish stating my name, he interjected me once more. This time his interruption was more intentional.

"Oh, I know who you are this isn't the first time we have met. However, I'm not entirely surprised you bare no memory of our first encounter, dearest Eva."

As he released my now ripe raw hands, I was pulled into an unusual memory of a dream, from when I was just a child. The dream had been one that I couldn't forget and I was about to find out why. I was crawling along this very floor as I glanced down, I recall trying my hardest to get to my feet. Aged only two, all I wanted was to catch a glimpse of the giant grey man, I laughed softly. This was no giant grey man and it certainly hadn't been a dream - it had been a memory stored deep in my subconscious young mind. I slowly nodded, now remember bragging about him to my classmates.

"That does seem so." I looked around the room with my new perspective, the memory becoming clearer. I crooked my head upward once again to look at the statue, my eyes applauding his face.

"May I ask you why you are here?" I queried inquisitively. "I am just like everything else; I only come to life once you enter the room. Not unlike the walls of your bedroom. I am able to transform into the figure you require, as a man I harbour the ability to communicate, do you wish to talk?" I tapped my chin, trying to wrap my head around his words. Although they made vague sense, I couldn't comprehend the fact he didn't really exist, just like in my infant imagination.

Cornelius I called him, having a name for him made his presence less surreal - he quickly became something of a comforter of mine. I finally had someone to call upon to help be bare my abundance of secrets, for endless hours I would sit, eat and sleep in the company of my new exclusive friend.

I suppose in a way he replaced the friend I had lost so long ago. Have you ever missed someone so much that you constantly replay each and every moment you spent together? Without Tyler, it almost felt like I wasn't really living, despite the fact I was now blessed with all the spender of my new home. Cornelius had made this alien place feel like home. Leaving Tyler behind wasn't a break up it was the ending of a beautiful chapter in my life, an obligation necessary to let a new tale begin. You have no idea how much I wish I could turn back the pages.

Cornelius could do something no one ever had done before, he understood me to an almost disturbing level. He was an extension of myself and without knowing it, he knew me just as well if not better than I knew myself. I badgered him with question after question. He may have been able to tap into my mind, but before me he was my grandmother's guardian, an invaluable history.

"Can, I ask you something?" Slowly, Cornelius nodded.

"Tell me about the first day I arrived here I want to know everything! Your memory is an archive of every person who has walked these floors including mine; I need to know everything that happened on that day, please?"

I waited.

"They never managed a honeymoon that fall." I frowned. "Everyone had gathered the entirety of the underworld had come to bear witness, the leader of Avalon finally branding the once stray wild young wonderer. Men and woman including those who simply admire your kind both mortal and otherwise, gathered in marvellous attendance. Very soon after the ceremony had finished and the cheers had silenced, a source told of your whereabouts and potential greatness, if properly nurtured. Hedwinn wanted to train you from the youngest age possible, to have you entered into the…"

He paused. "To summarise, he wanted you on side, he and Verdon left the ceremony and their guests moments after the announcement was made to the rest of the coven." I already knew the rest of the tale, my wise grandmother wasn't going to hand me over to some pale faced, possibly psychotic men. Even if they were wearing suites. "Christina, the wife, she didn't mind, she said nothing?" Cornelius managed a small smile. "You may not know by now but Christina is a very devoted wife, she knew the implications of the man whom she agreed to be tied to for the remainder of her existence. She understood his commitments and was patient."

I grinned as another piece of my broken memory was slotting into place but with my eyes watering with exhaustion. I was forced to wave a tired goodbye to Cornelius, I planned to return the next evening. As I left the room I thought about the likeness between the giant, and the toys I kept as a child, so alive to me but not to anyone else.

After much endurance I had found the door marking my name, I ran to the duvet and sat up in my large bed smiling as I noticed the vines over my bed had generously grown strawberries. I blushed as I got up onto my knees picking one carefully, I rolled the juicy fruit between my fingertips a few times placing the delicious red fruit to my lips and taking a bite as I did so I hungrily plucked another.

"I really should eat something more substantial." I may be half vampire but I needed excessive nutrients, nothing I plucked from the vines of any tree would provide the substance I truly needed. The headaches were excruciating. I pondered on what my life could have been like if a different coven had found me, I shuddered at that prospect.

Christina and I were undoubtedly the lucky ones.

# 4. FUN AND GAMES

I needed guidance, if only I could find out more about my grandmother *beyond the knowledge of Cornelius*, what would she do if she were in my shoes now? On the way to Avalon, Hedwinn wasn't exactly an open book when I asked him about her connection to the coven or mine for that matter. I could hardly imagine my mother or father having any idea that a world such as this existed. After all to them this would just be another tale of make believe and nonsense.

I knocked hysterically on Hedwinn's grand door which reeked of old pine wood I inhaled it with each passing breath. I was unsure of exactly what I would find behind the door. I had imagined Hedwinn would be the type to emerge himself in an impressive horde of books. I suspected he would most likely be the proud owner of an extensive collection of interesting, introvert and one of a kind artefacts, each one proudly on display.

I wasn't even close, as the door opened without aid I watched Hedwinn as he swung towards me like Tarzan across his enormous room using twisted vines he swung from side to side towards me, his room was bigger than our dining hall. He didn't even have a bed he barely owned one stick of practical furniture, just a single chest of locked wooden drawers - *pine probably.* I knew almost instantly that I had caught him at a bad time. As I twisted around to leave an arrow shot the door frame, making me jump, turning around I watched a chuckling Hedwinn leaping down to greet me his feet inches from mine, I folded my arms.

"Hedwinn, that was hardly appropriate, I could have been killed I hope you realise that!" I jokingly protested, his master suit made my room look like a dark hallow prison without life or soul, just solitary concrete frame, is this how he spent his free time? *Jesus.*

"Oh? Then I will be sure to try harder next time, I'm not known for having a terrible aim." He jested as I laughed until finally he asked. "What can I help you with?"

"I wanted to talk to you about my grandmother, I believe you are hiding something and I know with certainly I have been here before. My memories are fragile but by no means are they fictional, you can't tell me it's all coincidental. So please if there is anything, so much as the tiniest detail. I think I have a right to know about my past, don't you?"

Hedwinn had begun drying sweat off his bare shoulders with a grey towel he had pulled from a compartment which had just erected amongst the shrubbery. As I spoke his room had been morphing into a very clean, very pastel chamber much more of what I had expected. An office fit for the current governing figure of Avalon.

Together we walked over to one corner of the chamber where a set of chairs had emerged, beside a large window.

Everything had slowly formulated amongst what was remained of the trees.

Hedwinn and I both took a seat opposite the opening but I never allowed myself a moment's distraction from this conversation, despite the magnificent view - an illusion of blue sky. I wasn't allowing my questions to remain unanswered I knew that he was holding something back, I needed more.

"Our profiteer Harpitunia had told of a child that would one day find her way here, a child who needed to have the upbringing from Uppers before she could be changed, we were never shown images of you. Verdon made frequent visits to the locations we were given, one of which was your home where your grandmother would frequently attend.

"In order to see if the profiteer was correct we had Verdon bring you and your holder here. The moment you were brought into these halls it was abundantly clear that you were the child we had been informed about.

"We knew that once the time came you would be a great and valuable asset to our kingdom. This life has always been at the centre of your destiny Eva. Your grandmother all but insisted we give you a normal life, to later allow **you** to choose the path you wish to follow.

"I am gravely sorry that Julia robbed you of that choice. She always thought that since she was never given the option to choose this life it was unjust that you should be given that right automatically. She was born into this life but you were not, the concept of Uppers becoming one of us never truly sat right with Julia or Magnus. They would often talk about how little our kind needed civilians like you, in their mind unless you're born into this life you should not be 'given' it.

"She is a very emotionally driven narrow-minded woman with no sense of greater meanings. Somewhat like the individuals who brought you into this world.

"We gave your grandmother the pendant to keep, so that when the time came if you ever wanted to find us it would lead you here. We always knew we would find you wearing that blue pendant. I would like to think this is the life you would have chosen because I believe this is the right path - we are going to do some amazing things with you by our side Eva."

I smiled gratefully that Hedwinn had told me everything or at least he thought he needed to know. He was right after all, this is where I belong. The facts could not be questioned; Hedwinn was not responsible for the death of Tyler's brother, if we were given the chance to explain they would see the truth. I decided to leave Hedwinn to his workout, but as I made my way to the banquet hall. I thought about my grandmother and how my grandmother managed never to tell a soul about this world, not to a single person. Why was my having such a normal childhood such a necessity?

What had made her insist on a human childhood, when I could have been brought up in a world of grandeur and incredible role models? In reflection in my Upper life I had certainly learnt about modesty, then I thought about Tyler and I couldn't help but smile. He was certainly worth finding in the mortal life I was given.

Hedwinn and Verdon had disappeared, their full plates sat beside the occupied seats of the twins. This had been the first time I attempted to help prepare the evening meal; the cooked seasoned Crazors amounted to a great deal of effort, much more than any ordinary cut of chicken or lamb. Everything had gotten cold now; I tapped my impatient fingertips against the oak table as my annoyance mounted. Had they deliberately avoided this lunch at the risk that I'd under cook the food? I huffed.

*Unbelievable.* Even in Avalon rudeness was still rudeness wasn't it? I glanced over to a grinning Genevieve, her amusement was probably down to the fact my tapping fingers had begun indenting the wood. "You should have made extra." She suggested, a frown persisted between my brows as I pondered her untactful use of sarcasm when I was clearly already worked up.

"All 4 will return shortly, you'll see."

4? I looked around the table, counting each individual as I scoured, everyone accounted for accept the obviously missing two.

"They are bringing people back with them? No one told me we were having visitors." I replied to her as my brow creased further and my confusion grew.

"It's that time." She edged her chair towards me, the chairs legs barely scrapping the refined pristine floor. Whilst the other members of our coven including an unusually quiet Christina, polished their plates, Genevieve's voice was quieter than before as she spoke.

"I hear we have clutched ourselves two very strong souls with great potential, I can't wait to see what they each have to offer. Oh, I just **love** this time of the century! Kayleigh and I have already begun sketching out our outfits and yours, of course. I wonder what Verdon will name this pair, he lives for the adrenaline rush you get with good hearty competition."

I stared blankly at Genevieve as her animated lips kept speaking words I didn't understand - what did Verdon live for and who specifically were they bringing back?

Unlike me Morgan and Keira the pair in question, would have to compete for their right to a place as part of our coven. From the moment Verdon took them both eagerly beneath his experienced wing, the training had begun and the pressure had started to build. I thought Hedwinn was joking when he told me the complexities of the initiation process. In the company of everyone a slightly dubious Morgan and Keira swore an oath of loyalty on behalf of our coven, and its people, under the eyes of the ancestors. An oath to compete at the Annual Balistra Heritage extravaganza in our honour, the ball was held every century at the centre of the underground universe, the Balistra grounds.

The arena lay dormant for the majority of years between each decade, but for 3 spectacular days it was host to the most exclusive of events at which many trial members would compete for a chance to become one of us. It wasn't just about testing potential new members, it was about satisfying a deeper seeded competitive need of each covens leader. Every breed including the Phethlim, Gohinease and of course our tribe, The Triquils. Would be fighting for a chance to heighten their reputation and status as the most ferocious coven of all Avalon's inhabitants.

Every century the leaders of each coven selected two desirable civilians from the Upper world. They would be granted the opportunity to be trained by the leaders, and second in commands of each coven. If the fortunate applicant accepted they would then be injected with a small amount of the trainer's blood, over a short period of time, giving them the temporary extraordinary abilities. Each unique to the individual, the natural abilities of the person would be amplified by the blend of Crazors blood, and the blood of the powerful leader. The outcome was often deadly.

It was compulsory for the hopefuls to prove they could handle the change throughout their training, but more importantly the individual would have to succeed in the battle. In order for the change to be made permanent. Hedwinn later told me trails of previous applicants who became obsessed with power, and some who completely lost every ounce of their humility, the sudden blast of power would often result in cases such as Luciana's.

It was thought that very few civilians harboured suitable genetic ingredients, that could be converted into what were essentially supernatural abilities; I prayed for our specially selected applicants. Both Morgan and Keira had taken to the training so effortlessly, both had begun developing an impressive multitude of talents which had already started strengthening with every harrowing training session. Put it this way, I certainly wouldn't want to fight against either of them and I was grateful I wouldn't have to.

On one of my rare vacant afternoons, I would sneak to the south quarter to watch the intense training. Inspecting their progress after which I would often report back to an eager set of twins. Kayleigh in particular was extremely excitable to learn of Morgan's progression.

Every competitor who was chosen to represent each coven at the Balistra heritage ball was given a mere 3 months to prepare. In the small quarters the contenders had everything they needed, including a generous supply of Crazors blood to keep their strength up, and an endless amount of time with both Hedwinn and Verdon. I was often amazed by Verdon's particular dedication to the cause, he would often skip meal times to help them both develop, together and independently.

After a few spying sessions I started to understand the reason why not one person, had conceived a child within Avalon. Not only were the candidates a potential danger to themselves and but they required so much nurturing and if neither of them were successful, our coven would be subjected to ridicule.

Thankfully the unsuccessful candidates would have their memories erased by the powerful Thomas, robust leader of the Phethlim tribe. Once his or her memory of the underworld was no longer in existence, Verdon would take the bewildered pair back to the surface. It was tragic ultimately barbaric.

I was assured that no physical contact would be allowed during the battle, Morgan, Keira and the competitors would have to rely on their harboured alibies if they stood any chance of winning. For Morgan that ability was generating incredible illusions; he was very much a trickster with a range of frightful tactics up his sleeve. He had the potential to completely disorient his competitors, he could manifest their biggest fear based on his initial analysis of his competition. I wasn't entirely sure of Keira's ability just yet, I had only spotted her training once or twice, she was usually found busting punching bags to smithereens and flying her way through countless agility tests. Not literally *unfortunately*.

The twins informed me the only way you can win the battle is by forcing the other competitors to mercifully surrender, at least it wasn't death. One thing which hindered the entire progress was the complete lack of knowledge on all sides, we had no idea who the other tribes had chosen.

There is absolutely no telling what our trainees could be up against until one by one they step into the stadium. This crucially meant that every possibility had to be adhered and trained for. Whether that is someone who could render themselves invisible or even a personable to regenerate otherwise known as healing themselves, everything needed to be pre-empted. It was mindboggling.

It was often torturous to think about this ash haired, blue eyed and broad shouldered teen rouge boy. Alongside our beautiful sweet auburn haired, freckled girl going up against someone who could by now be at any skill level. I couldn't escape the sickening thought that this was the very purpose Julia had changed me all those months ago, she wanted to train me. To make me like her, to have me fight against strangers to gain her nothing greater than cowardice *honour*.

If things had gone her way she desired to train me to kill without mercy or fear, it would have always been a suicide mission. One in which her finger would not be lifted. If she was ever to suffer the slightest ounce of pain, my ability would have surely been tested. I would have literally fought her battles, then subsequently healed myself. Though I'm not sure that's even possible, death would have been a merciful gift at the end of her reign.

Fortunately Verdon was very experienced, he had an understanding of which areas needed development with each pair. He knew precisely how to strengthen their weaknesses, but most importantly he was able to play to their existing strengths. Their joint youthful age would certainly give them an undeniable edge over anyone older, against Hedwinn's advice I wanted to befriend them both. I felt compelled to give them both an equal reason to fight. I knew more than most how it felt to be isolated even in a place as welcoming as Avalon.

Meeting our competitors for first time was certainly an unusual experience. It wasn't until one week until the battle that I finally managed to interact with both of them. Surprisingly it was under Hedwinn's unexpected invitation. Verdon wasn't allowing for any distractions for the duo however he couldn't let his duties fall by the waste side, he did have other priorities.

For each competitor at least one trainer was required to be present at all times, Verdon was required to make his routine checks of the portals. In his absence Hedwinn had requested I assist him in supervising the training, to gain some experience. I couldn't have been more torn about the idea of finally being given the opportunity to help, I could hardly bear the thought of injuring myself further not with the Balistra trip just around the corner. Never the less I was flattered to be asked at all, I kindly accepted his request.

As I stepped over the threshold the chill swept past my arms and raised the hairs which lay there, this certainly was the most neglected part of Avalon. Perfect for young applications with a certain tendency to break inanimate objects including their bones. As I took several more steps forward I could hear the panting, grunting and yelling all stemming from Hedwinn's domineering demands to the exhilarated pair.

"Fear will paralyse you, terror will distract your senses but bravery will free your minds to find strength and answers."

The instructions echoed louder through the halls, bouncing against every angle, as I headed into the last archway. The scent of sweat, testosterone and electric energy hit me like a wave of glorious sunshine I was dying to bathe in. Hedwinn stripped of his usual overcoat and wore a fitting grey shirt and black trousers, I watched as he stood talking to Keira. Looking around the room I could have sworn the many mirrors were playing tricks on me.

As one Keira walked towards me another two kicked, jumped and weaved through hot burning coals. The scent of which threw aside the other more appealing fragrances in the air. I stared with confusion as she stepped closer, was this another one of Morgan's illusions or have I lost my mind? I couldn't tell, it was awe strikingly marvellous.

"Amazing isn't it? I have only managed to multiply myself a maximum of 4 times since starting this process but I'm pushing for at least 5! It's exhausting but it swings the odds my way."

I was truly mesmerised with her ability of self-duplication, if she managed to fully master her skill in time she could be in with a real chance of becoming our victor.

"What can you do?" I heard a brash Morgan ask, I stepped to one side to answer his question revealing myself from behind Keira to answer.

"I'm a healer." I smiled

"You can heal yourself? Christ that's incredible! No wonder you made it." I smiled again with a little less enthusiasm.

"Not exactly." He frowned, but before I could respond Hedwinn quickly interrupted. "We are going hunting today."

"*Hunting*?" My voice squeaking with fright.

"This challenge will put your skills of endurance to the test. Verdon has informed me the land surrounding one of the Circus tree patches is clear of Uppers this afternoon. He has planted 7 items of value amongst the nearby land. To help you find them they have all been coated in a generous layer of Crazors blood. You will both have to utilise the tracking, restraint and mostly importantly the agility tricks we have taught you. If you are to succeed in the race, and I am expecting a speedy return.

"I will accompany Keira and her clones whilst Eva will follow Morgan. The timer will start the moment we all land, once all 7 goods have successfully been collected we will return to the tree. No diversions or exceptions. If you're faced with a competitor with the ability to strip you of your powers you will need to rely on your very basic instincts, so do not underestimate them. Follow me."

I walked beside Hedwinn with a smile on my face, as much as the competitors did I too needed a break from the walls which had now surrounded me for what felt like years. As we reached the Circus tree both mine and Hedwinn's pendants shone.

I joined hands with Keira and Hedwinn the instant we were all swallowed into the portal to the Uppers world. Both competitors hit the ground with a thump. Unable to hold my balance I also tumbled down with them, but I quickly jumped to my feet and grabbed the arm of Morgan, pulling his mangled body from the ground.

"You want to win don't you? **Get up, come on let's go!**" I pulled him from the earth leaving a weary Keira behind, although I wasn't technically taking part in the challenge it had ignited my competitive nature. My senses immediately highlighted the locations at which two of the closest treasures were located, the aroma of which was carried through the easterly breeze.

I had forgotten for a moment that Morgan was not yet a full blooded member of our kind. I charged forward and, forcefully I stopped myself after a couple of mile to allow him the chance to catch up. As I waited, my heart sluggishly thumped in my chest adrenaline pumping through my body, a wealth of life surrounding me.

The songs of birds filtering down through the colourful tree branches, I could hear the voice of Hedwinn not far behind adding blissful comfort to the relaxing environment.

Morgan was now ahead of me I smiled and followed after him, I couldn't help but laugh as he bustled his way between the branches surrounding us, his senses leading him in entirely the wrong direction, he was overthinking every step. Blinded by glory.

"Stop." I hailed and stood beside him.

"Close your eyes and just breathe, this is the most natural instinct any member of our kind can call upon. Shut your mind off and focus on breathing."

Without a word he followed my guidance and closed his eyes, his previously hunched shoulders relaxed for a few seconds before he rushed off in the correct direction. I grinned and began running behind him with pride and excitement, coursing through my body simultaneously. Much to our disappointment Keira has reached the emeralds stone before us. She was quick to let us know her clones were already hunting out the other items, but Morgan was even quicker to shoot past us all.

I darted behind his tracks and before I knew it I had caught up, now running with ease beside him. I grinned in the knowledge that we were already close to another treasure within seconds of him successfully picking up the scent.

I watched bemused as Morgan dived to the ground as though he was about to score the final try at the rugby world cup final. A loud thump broke through the trees as Morgan leaped to grab the diamond from a decrepit branch. I took the Crazors blood covered jewel and stuffed it into my pocket in the hope the scent of it wouldn't act as a distraction, as we hunted out more of the items. Before I knew it he was off again. Almost knocking me to the ground, heading towards a river we could hear flowing nearby.

As we shot past two of Keira's clones searching through the wilderness. Whilst running I glanced over between the wilderness to give Hedwinn a reassuring smile as he followed behind her, suddenly Morgan stopped right at the river's violent edge.

"He can't be seriously expecting us to jump over that."

I looked down over the edge, Verdon must have drenched this area in Crazors blood. The intoxicating scent of it lingered on the back of my thirsty throat with each inhale, the trail had me salivating until Morgan grabbed my attention.

"Just over there!" I followed his pointed finger to a nest of speckled red Crazors eggs, each of them submerged within the rocks over the other side of the river. "Swing me!" I frowned and responded to his idiocy. "Do what?"

"Swing me, grab my hand swing me around, let go at the correct moment. I'll land right over on the other side."

I laughed. "What are you? A swing ball?" He laughed just as hard as I did, I knew I could physically do it but I wasn't so confident in his landing abilities combine that with my imbalance.

It was likely we were about to have a disaster on our hands, it would have been more logical for him to have thrown me, but it wasn't my job to collect the treasures. After a couple of moments of deliberation I allowed my competitive nature to overpower, my sense of reasoning and logic I certainly wasn't about to give up.

But I didn't want to be the one responsible for him losing his first challenge and mine for that matter. I grabbed his wrist. "You had better land more accurately than you did when we arrived here!" Without a second thought I grabbed his wrist tighter and we began spinning, faster and faster almost immediately everything around us had become a stream of colour all combining as one never ending cycle.

Once his feet had lifted from the ground I felt his weight tugging me from left to right, I swung faster until the opportune moment had arrived, like a shot - he flew up into the air.

I closed my eyes and waited for him to either splash into the river or hit the ground *hard*. For those few seconds I thought about how furious Hedwinn would be if I injured one of our competitors by throwing him into a river, my eyes shot open. I watched breathlessly as Morgan rolled onto the grass way over on the other side of the river. I grinned at our success, no healing necessary.

As he walked towards the edge I could hear Keira's feet fast approaching Morgan must have heard her too, as he stepped one foot into the current to inch closer to the nest. He clung to a rock for support as he leant closer and closer, finally his hand met the nest. I paused as he rummaged through the eggs and pulled out a small marble figure resembling Cornelius from between them. He threw it over to me and to my surprise I actually managed to catch it; I placed it in my now full pockets. Hedwinn and a victorious Keira arrived just in time to help Morgan make his was back across the river; Hedwinn has packed an emergency set of equipment to aid him, luckily he didn't need more than a towel.

"3 out of 4, that's not bad. Don't be disheartened." I heard him say to Morgan as he pulled him up from the rivers bank.

Although we had lost the challenge I think overall Morgan had displayed the most varied rage of skills, after all it was practically 4 against 1. I handed all of our small trophies to Hedwinn who carried them in his pockets, with nothing but Crazors blood running through our minds hungrily we all headed back to the circus tree. Keira took this opportunity to walk beside me.

"Hedwinn rarely smiles does he?" I laughed. "There's a lot to play for next week, it's certainly nothing personal so don't worry." An anxious smile crossed her face

"He won't always be like this." I smiled we entered back into the spacious quarters; sweat was coating Morgan's pale skin as he turned to look at me. "Eva." He said my name whilst cleaning his hand with a towel as he walked towards me, I shook his hand and grinned.

"Morgan, I'd just like to congratulate you on your performance today, and to wish you good luck next week as I doubt I'll see you again before then. Verdon doesn't take to well to interferences but sometimes too much of one thing can do more harm than good."

He grinned a wide toothy grin, as though warmed by my words, he took a seat at his warn bench press.

"I couldn't agree more." He smiled as I leant against the wall. I knew it wouldn't be a good move to allow myself to become attached to someone who may or may not be here next week, but I couldn't help but sympathise.

"Do you think you're ready?" It took a while for him to respond to my question, but then he released a heavy sigh. "I think so; I can't put into words how much I want this, to belong to something so unique. I will fight to the death, or until a series of surrenders, whatever comes first."

I didn't know what to say, his determination was awesome. A true testament to the time our leaders had bestowed on him.

"What about you?" He enquired. "I hear you are the guest of honour at the ball, that's exciting isn't it?" I had forgotten about that, the ball was a 3 day celebration, which began with a huge banquet. During the event each coven would raise a toast to their great, and honourable leaders. Afterwards each leader would then hail the ancestors. It would be around this point that I would have to be introduced to everyone; I knew each introduction would be more excruciating then the last. I wasn't good at making valuable first impressions.

"I suppose, you have more to worry about so keep your eye on the prize." I chuckled and crept my way back to my room, chewing over the events to come.

The ball gave the twins yet another excuse to dress me up in an excessive costume, my every curve was squeezed into a tight corset. I didn't know that suffocation was part and parcel of looking conventionally pretty, but apparently it was. At least I wasn't the only one suffering both the twins and Christina were sporting similar ensembles; Aluma was the only one exempt from wearing the gown, the fact that she didn't have to wear it made her grateful for her age. A feeling I gathered was somewhat unusual for her.

No matter how many times I looked in the mirror in the twins' bedroom, I couldn't believe that the woman looking back, was actually me. Although, I was reminded of myself when I fell over the dresses small train as I took the dress off. The next time I would be wearing it will be at the ball itself. I wasn't exactly thrilled about being the 'newbie' at such a prestigious event. I had to admit all the preparation was a welcome distraction from missing Tyler all the time and, distressing about the battle. Awkward buttons and lace had taken over my agenda of worries now.

The twins didn't have to worry, they were already intrigued into the preceding's; they already knew the routine, and were excited for the occasion. I suppose wasn't completely clueless, I have been to my fair share of weddings, birthday parties and anniversaries, but I have always preferred the more personal approach to celebrating milestones. A well selected playlist, a bottle of wine, a camera to capture the event and of course a few close relatives to celebrate with. That was my idea of a stress free party.

It wasn't long until my birthday; I hoped that my new friends knew me well enough not to plan a lavish soiree to mark the date. I hadn't even attended my high school prom to avoid the hustle and bustle, large crowds always made me nervous; the build-up to this gathering was all too familiar to the prom set up only this time I couldn't back out.

Maybe it wouldn't be as bad as I imagined various conflicting breeds all confined under one roof, what could possibly go wrong? I didn't dare ask that out loud I didn't want to tempt fate into answering that cautious question. In the grander scheme of things, the opening ceremony would be the easy part, the battle would be a mere few hours away and our pride and people would be at stake.

Not participating at all could be misinterpreted as me snubbing the traditions of our world, I didn't want to be the cause of upset and start relations on a sour note. The candidates wouldn't be invited to the introductory ritual; you had to be a fully-fledged member of one of the covers to be guaranteed a place. I wonder how far word of my arrival had spread, I hoped the words of me were kind if nothing else.

When I allowed myself to stop and think about things rationally, everything was moving so quickly, it felt as though in one second I was just Eva. But now, I had transformed into Miss Evangeline Carter - the newest, youngest and arguably the most controversial member of the Triquils clan. If it wasn't for my history and Harpitunia's prediction, I would be in Morgan's shoes... I didn't even want to imagine it. The cloak had told the final hour, it was time; it was as though someone had pressed fast forward on the remote controlling my life, and they weren't about to let go.

\*\*\*\*\*

Stood in the grand entrance to historically dazzling Balistra, dressed like a prom queen stood beside my sisters in dresses and, my bothers in suits. I was overwhelmed by the use of blistering gold furnishings. Unlike our home, the circus tree was at the heart of the grounds, no walls or windows to hide an embarrassing fall. Luckily, in heels I just about stood my ground, until ushered aside by Hedwinn as other covens and lone vampires made their graceful entrances.

The new faces were awe crushingly beautiful, everyone dressed as through ready for a meeting with the queen, I suppose each leader is the Uppers equivalent of royalty. The other men and women swooped in like birds of prey, landing with precision in front of us, we certainly weren't in Kansas anymore. The only familiarity I could find between here and home was above our heads. This building also had no roof in which to shelter us from the elements. Unlike our Triquil home this roof invited in a zoo of enthralling and exotic creatures; both big and small. Tonight we were all guests in their permanent home. Absolutely everything glistened - is this what limitless expenditure could bring?

The solid pathway we all walked upon was beautifully hand painted, as I stepped inside I thought about how even Michael Angelo would have been envious of this exquisite work. The masterful paintings featuring the anguished faces of two bearded men one about to tackle the other, with what looked like a bloody spear. A crowd of teary young and old faces gathered around the pair, battle scared and bruised bodies both about to collapse, but neither willing.

The deeper into Balistra we travelled the more powerful my feelings became that I didn't belong within these luxurious walls. I stuck close to Hedwinn throughout the introductory evening, the noises surrounding us was deafening with glasses of various blood types crashing together, men from other covens had set up various small gatherings amongst themselves. They were all proving their strengths with arm wrestling, tree crushing and even rib crushing, I clasped my hand over my mouth as vomit tried to force its way up my throat and into my mouth. I was sickened at myself for salivating over the delicious scent of copper blood, I was positively weeping.

If that wasn't enough to set me reeling not only was I alluded by the smell of food, blood and people in the air, but the animals which had inhabited the building were also toying with my senses. In this room almost everything was considered a meal.

I continued to wander behind as Hedwinn confidently strolled towards large crowds of various breeds, Hedwinn spoke to one person after another. Although I was trying to remember the names, my concentration was diverted. Needing to pay particular attention to exactly where I placed my feet, with so many creatures passing by my ankles. Tiny adorable lion cubs running alongside crocodiles and minute lady bugs, all of the creatures had wandered in through the various cracks and entry points scattered around the ancient building. Shadows cascaded over the many beautifully marked faces in the room and as I looked up, I found the source.

Hungry eagles with mice squealing between their beaks and colourful parrots flew overhead, creating a mirage of yellow, red and green. The branches of the trees from outside were overhanging into the building, the twigs cluttered with nests of new born birds and squirrels. The wild animals had made Ballista their home in our absence; it was a breath-taking contrast to the stone structure imagined.

I glanced away from the view as forthcoming footsteps had diverted my attention. I looked up at the unsuspecting man. I couldn't help but smile at what he was holding, another new born lion cub. I reached out and stroked the lion between its two big beautiful eyes, its ears and paws twitching.

The cub began licking my finger, its rough tongue the replica of pin pricks against my skin. The man began to speak. "Lion cubs are so precious and rare these days, almost as *cute* as they're delicious."

I frowned my stomach already churning with the words he had spoken, pulling back my hand as I caught him inspecting my obviously visible marking. I instantly felt uncomfortable beneath his stare, the man had toned arms and dark skin which complimented his black eyes. I noticed his ear piercing just above his bold marking which grew from his shoulder to his throat. My inspection was intermittent as he spoke again.

"E! My you've grown up, truly remarkable at last your kind has manage to achieve something with substance, if you do not mind my saying so." E? I was uncharacteristically speechless; he shook my shoulder and grinned wickedly.

"The legend ceases to be true - it is about time." I nodded gawkily unable to take my eyes away from the cub he was still holding, I wasn't deliberately trying to be rude. I just didn't want to say something I would inevitably regret, so it was better to say nothing. If I opened my mouth who knows what secrets might fall out, I didn't want to give anything away for both our opponents and my coven's sake.

"I am Barasa, leader of the Gohinease tribe." I shook his hand and met his eyes to smile.

"I wish my darling mate had been here to see this, she will never believe me. Will you be attending the slaughtering tomorrow?"

My previously relaxed arms folded over my exhaling chest and my eyes automatically narrowed.

"I will be there to see our competitors initiating their competition, if that's what you mean?"

Up until this point, I didn't think I cared too much for the battle itself, but I had become both defensive and competitive, it was completely infectious police- I wanted the pride, I wanted it for myself but most of all I wanted it for Hedwinn and Verdon. They had worked too hard to leave with anything less than a satisfying victory, on the other hand I suppose I really have been spending too much time in their company. Their nature was becoming mine.

"That's what we like to have, a fighting spirit at last. Although I must confess, it is still a mystery to me as to why you name your lessors. Nonetheless I, my mate, 1772 and 1773 will be seeing you tomorrow for the initiation - it will be our pleasure." He mocked.

"Ugh." I groaned as he strode towards one of the many gatherings of men, I tried to shake away the sour taste he had left in my mouth. If nothing else the conversation fuelled my desire to win. More importantly, I had started to feel a true sense of allegiance and devotion towards my coven. I wanted more than ever to prove that we are the elite breed in more ways the one.

When it came time for us all to take our places around the huge dining table, I was given the honour of a seat at the south side, directly opposite Thomas. The robust Phethlim leader who took pride of place as the last victor in the Balistra battles, he squeezed into his seat which dwarfed those around him. The chair was carved with the names and faces of our ancestors' and previous tournament victors initials engraved into the wood, a gift to each champion.

Even before everyone had taken their places, Thomas had already chomped down several of the human eye balls marinated in blood, in a bowel he had situated before him, the man certainly had an insatiable appetite. I tried my best not to look as he wiped his blood red lips with a white cloth. My body shrieked as he chewed, cracked and crunched one eye ball at a time. As a desperate distraction, I observed everyone getting reacquainted around the polished to perfection table, filling up their glasses and straightening out their cutlery.

Birds and fellow woodland creatures flew overhead, neither had dared to take a bite of the generous selection of food. It felt like an unspoken truth that any greedy creature would themselves become part of tonight's feast, should they become a nuisance.

The itself food had been strategically placed; the human meat was closest to the Phethlim and the Gohinease tribesman, much to Thomas' delight.

The selection of sustenance included everything from boiled fingers and raw cuts of shoulder. At the centre of the table laid a delicious human heart, the scent of which saturated the air. Around the table the only hearts truly beating were the ones of my fellow Triquils. The further along the able towards myself looked, the less appetising the food became I looked down to the nearest bowl to me Crazors blood soup. I tried my best to imagine the appetising heart as not only a *person* which represented a personality, a human, a life but s someone I knew. It made my tasteless soup that much easier to swallow.

The elephant in the room was written on the faces of my coven's members, but no more so than mine. I looked over to Hedwinn, indulged in conversation with Verdon, most likely conversing about tomorrow's battle. I cringed as my foot was kicked by Genevieve who sat to my left she wasn't too pleased my lack of optimism in relation to talking others.

My eyes narrowed, it was difficult to start conversation when all you can hear is the constant smacking of Thomas' lips. I had no desire to get acquainted with that particular man; much to my disappointment the feeling of disinterest wasn't mutual. His loud voice was easily carried across the crowed and nosy table, one by one heads turned in my direction as he spoke.

"Young one, you're going to need your strength, defeat will be bitter pill to swallow."

I never wanted to be the source of an uncomfortable atmosphere but through no fault of my own I found myself the subject of several stares. I kept my eyes down as my spoon circled in the soup I tried to conjure a response witty enough, once the one liner popped into my head I looked up and met Thomas' gawping face. A smile on my dry lips.

"Defeat is a state of mind, I however gain my strength from somewhere other than my gut, my soul serves me well."

A toothy grin spread on the faces of my fellow coven members, contrary to the man directly opposite me. The existence of my soul was still a very real possibility, contrasting his. I smirked as his eyes never wavered from mine, had he finally lost his appetite? Reaching for a large Crazor, I tore a leg with my cut-throat piercing teeth and placed it to my starved lips devouring the meat, as the Gohinease leader Barasa chuckled to himself along with the twins. I was given the impression that not many stood up against Thomas and I don't think he appreciated my high-handed response. Unlike the members of his cowardice coven I wasn't about to be walked over, certainly not by a blind ignoramus.

I ate until the straps of my red coursed became too tight around my waist, unable to use my lungs to full capacity I took short quick breaths until I was shown to the humungous Triquil quarters for the night.

The walls here were unchanging; I had become accustom to my virtual assistant. Tiny cracks in the otherwise spotless room allowed me to peek into my neighbouring suit, identical to my own. The roof overhead was extremely draftee; it didn't correspond at all with the huge dining area. I suppose these rooms were barely used for sleeping, for practicality they were designed to house those who could not feel the goose pimples these thin walls created. A humming bird flew down to the headboard of my huge if not slightly uncomfortable bed, its sung kept me company as I tried to pre-empt the best scenario for tomorrow.

I thought about Morgan, sweet Keira, and the other damned competitors for them returning home was as good as certain. I couldn't imagine returning to the other world, especially without the memories of the last 3 months of your life, without any recollection of Avalon and what you could have had. In one hand not being able to remember would be a blessing and in the other it was cruel to be robbed of  the choice, but if the exposure of our world become too much in the cities capital we would be inundated with applicants all in search of a better life.

To most people Avalon, Balistra and the inhabiting vampires are entirety is nothing more than an urban myth. Created to scare children into staying indoors or in groups whilst outside their communities. Only specially selected contacts knew the truth about us, about our life and more importantly - they knew our faces.

Verdon always caused a stir whilst visiting the Uppers, he is after all a strangely beautiful man, and I wouldn't be surprised if his sketch was up in a few police stations. The man always seen at the scene of disappearances every other decade - exposure spells trouble.

# 5. LET THE BALISTRA BATTLE BEGIN

I could barely hear my quick conspicuous steps on the decorative floor amongst the short silences between the cheers bellowing from the arena. Desperately searched for someone, anyone from my coven. The humongous swamp of unfamiliar faces had my hands shaking by my sides and sweat forming at my brow. Standing by a procession of strangers with beautiful faces; I knew I should keep my nose out of other people's business but, I just couldn't help but listen in to the huddle of men with brash voices stood to my far left.

They weren't just *men*; these were the second and third in commands. Each taking bets on the outcome and not one of them bared a single limitation, the only second in command not in attendance was Verdon. I knew both he and Hedwinn would be stood beside a very nervous Morgan and Keira right about now, for a last minute pep talk.

I leant in a little closer to listen to the men, just trying to get some idea of exactly who they were sending into the arena to fight, but the men were only concerned with wagers and they certainly weren't betting money as it held no profit in this world. Of course each one of them betting for the most valuable of constituents; areas of land. Both within and outside of Avalon, those who existed on human flesh were notorious for clashing over territories.

To them the Upper world was one mass mouth-watering hunting ground, with a growing population. Each man was convinced their coven had the winning competitor waiting in the wings.

I stood in amazement as the priceless bets were made, strangers boasting about their existent ownership on the Upper ground. I couldn't help myself from listening in to their fascination conversation until unexpectedly a young unfamiliar female voice resounded through the grounds with a gust of wind.

**"Ladies and Gentlemen please take your seats, the legendary Balistra battle is beginning!"** I almost leapt from my skin as the hairs raised on my arms with the sheer shriek of excitement in her voice. The announcement had triggered an army of excited people to swarm into the separate designated entrances.

Everyone except for the huddle of men who were utterly lost in their frivolous conversation ran towards the stands. I waited for the pandemonium to subside in order for me to find my seat. I continued cautiously stepping ever closer to the second in commands, waiting for the stampede to pass.

"I hear Barasa's 1772 can has mastered the ability to enhance or even weaken the powers of others if we are lucky, it's going to be a blood bath." I clenched my aching jaw.

"No, No. He's a man of extreme endurance it would take an army of elephants to take him down. Trust me the others don't stand a chance, come on. Let's up the stakes-I'll bet you the entire Scottish border!"

A middle aged man chuckled an almost childlike laugh, I got the feeling this man didn't get many opportunities to laugh or enjoy himself. He was relishing every second of the conversation. His clean but bone dry hands twisting together his eyes widened with excitement, he managed to persuade the men into taking his fruitless bets, idiots.

My fists clenched stiff at my sides my knuckles whitening with concern, observing more carefully at the men's faces. I couldn't help but notice how strikingly similar they all looked, it was so obvious I'm surprised I hadn't spotted it sooner. Their faces were all chiselled to perfection, every beautiful face had pronounced cheek bones, black hair and off putting bleak tired ragged completions. Deep bags laying lightly beneath their eyes due to stress I would imagine, certainly not due to a lack of sustenance. Apart from the mound of fleshy tissue beneath their eyes, the men bared no signs of aging. Not one wrinkle between them. Each individual had incredibly straight postures bearing strong arms.

For beings with such underling differences, they even wore the exact same rustic black ankle length jackets, tied at the centre exactly the same attire Hedwinn and Verdon. The more I thought about it they all fitted the description of henchmen. Beneath the long jackets were black shirts with grey buttons, those familiar Ted Baker boots were laced together. If you were to see them on the Upper surface in a dark ally, their appearance wasn't exactly deceptive.

The pastel faces were always hungry never satisfied, it seeped from their retched pours and more so through mine. As I glanced down towards their feet I was hit with a shocking revelation, Avalon was entirely without a female spearhead. Every leader and every second in command was male, my feeling of anger was replaced with one of sickness. I promised myself I would have to speak out about the injustice at the first opportune moment. Of the 5 men who stood within the menace circle; one man was remaining quiet I had to hold back a frightful gasp as our eyes met.

His skin was horrifically cracked around the corners of his mouth, his eyes bleak with a lifeless expression on his face not to mention he was excruciatingly thin. I couldn't bear to look at his painful existence for another moment longer. An unfamiliar voice to my right took me by surprise as she started to speak.

"That's Rhena." I glanced to the red headed woman and nodded, my staring had not gone unnoticed she too must have had the same idea about waiting behind to let the herd pass by before heading inside.

"Second leader of the Gohinease right?" The woman smiled.

"Not quite, he is a solo traveller, he is most noble and one of the bravest of our kind. Incredibly he manages to survive on plants, berries and other natural fruits alone, its suicide if you ask me."

Simultaneously between her speaking and my turning around I noticed her marking. There was only one other individual I had met who bared an identical marking as this, and as I thought about that person he walked over from the circle.

"I see you've met my mate at last; E this is my mate Fiona." I hugged her wearily, cautiously, I instantly regretted wrapping my arms around her so tightly. I could feel her inhaling against the dip between my shoulder and throat as she wrapped her arms around me, and I pulled back.

"I'm Eva, it's nice to meet you." His protective arm wrapped around her slender body as she spoke again.

"Oh, I know who you are, never the less we have no time for introductions sweetheart we best be getting to our seats. Good luck to the Triquils, Hedwinn and particularly your two competitors."

I took a sobering breath and found my way to our stand with the help of beautiful Fiona. I waved her goodbye and began taking the final steps to the viewing area for our coven. I smiled as familiar voices were introduced - at last I felt at home again. Back with my own kind, the people who believed as I did, with individuals I understood and trusted.

The view down to the battle field was excruciatingly intimate, looking across the arena I could see the euphoric faces of our rivals. At this distance I was able to witness the coven squabbling over large platters containing lumps of human flesh. Each of them like beasts they gulped down bright red and still warm blood. Height was the only thing which stood between the competitors and ourselves.

A confident Hedwinn strode into the stand, taking a seat between Christina and I, his demeanour was contagious. Our competitors are strong, they have been training together relentlessly, and we needed this. Gripping the corner of my chair leaning forward to get a better more precise view. The battle ground was covered in a white talcum surface, the stands decorated with each coven's markings. Flags flying high baring the initials of each coven's leader, barely readable in the strong easterly wind howling around the stadium.

The sound of bolts unhinging had everyone's attention, the door opposite us began to swing open, the previously electric chats from the crowd silenced. After a few agonisingly long seconds a shirtless man appeared. Behind him followed another, both men had biceps defined enough to lift up an army of men. Their hair tied back, crouching before one another as though already waiting to tear one another apart, the two never refrained eye contact. Fighting against someone who could potentially take the one open spot in your desired coven was the warrior you had trained with. The preparation process gave no alternative to fighting against someone you've become close with, training together exposed weaknesses.

The second pair to enter was welcomed with a deafening roar so powerful, my feet vibrated against the floor, shaking my knees and the chair beneath me. It was obvious the first pair had been trained by Barasa as his followers hailed as they approached the centre.

The pulsations from the Phethlim tribe was electric, shaking the area and every anxious warrior within it. My stomach churned as two new competitors appeared to be much younger than the first competitors who entered, the first men were at best twenty 5 years old.

The first woman surrounded by the crowed of men made her entrance. The young woman didn't show fear on her ivory face. The Gohinease coven applauded wildly for her and she lapped up the attention. Everyone else corralled in disbelief at the girl with slick long blond tied back hair. She too was agonizingly thin; it was painful to look at her frail body beside the fiercely muscular men. I knew she bared no hope, I couldn't contain my grief knowing Keira and Morgan were next to enter.

A couple of seconds later both our competitors entered, we all rose to our feet and cheered till our throats ached and our ears popped; I threw my fist into the air and stamped my feet repeatedly almost snapping my ankle in the process. Once all 6 applicants corrugated into a circle, with racing hearts we all took to our seats. Every breath felt like razor blades against the back of my now stinging throat.

As the 6 candidates circled one another, we were all silently questioning who would be brave or equally stupid enough to make the first move. Tension struck boiling point the ground began to shake, creating huge cracks from the centre of the battle field. Already impatient heckles tumbled down from the highest stands, the growing anxiety and anger collided together like nails down a chalkboard.

The Gohinease woman grinned a wicked smile, with a flick of the hand she flung the male Phethlim competitors against the enclosure. One remained concussed for a moment but the other did not falter; he landed perfectly on his feet, the crowd cheered at his bravery. With only a few cuts and bruises the man strutted towards the woman and suddenly her posture changed as they both locked eyes on one another, as he reached into his pocket she did the same.

I swallowed the thick lump in my throat, every step, every blink he made was projected onto her and with that it became 2 vs. 6. Assessing every move Morgan stood aside watching the pair who were now stalking towards him, mine and Morgan's' eyes locked for a moment.

Across the other side of the playing field the man had regained his consciousness and, turned his attention to Keira, she needed just 3 seconds to regenerate. Before she was given that opportunity the Phethlim man closed his eyes, Keira began to choke. Her preciously flawless skin tone was developing black spots, he was poisoning her body from the inside out. Every organism of the human within her was slowly being consumed. Her tiny hairs covering her body began to sizzle, her entire body wilted.

The man killing her grew weaker, Keira's body was strong enough to hold him off just long enough that when he was finished with her he also fell to the ground. Keira's body was reduced to nothing greater then a pile ash. Although I knew she would be reconstructed once the battle was over, watching her die left irreversible scares on my memory. I repeatedly asked those above to allow the ground to guzzle our remaining competitor up. I couldn't bear to see another person meet the same horrifying end.

As much as I hated this, I couldn't close my eyes for a millisecond, in hindsight, I am very glad I didn't. At that very moment Morgan's anger hit overdrive, his powers of illusion set the ground alight. Fire burned up from the ground it clung to the remaining pairs clothes surrounding them in a powerful blaze of smoke.

The man could no longer control the woman without heavy strain on his ability. Not when he couldn't see her properly, genius. Morgan jumped and clung to the bottom of our stand for the perfect view, from here he could twist his illusion to greater depths. The bewildered pair tried to escape the flames, although our coven knew the flames were just the trick of a talented illusionists. To the other competitors the fire was very real, and they were about to be engulfed. Morgan extended the fire to overwhelm the other covens, forcing them to become props in his game of make-believe.

The other male was weakened already from his control over the female, I jumped from my seat as the sound of Morgan's imagined gun fire and explosions tore through the sound barrier. I covered my ears as the perplexed competitors fell to the floor as Morgan focused his illusions on them Blasphemy was being screamed from the competing sides. Verdon stood with his arms folded grinning with pride as Morgan tortured the other two remaining souls.

The fire was closing in on the pair, giving them the impression they were about to be burnt to smithereens. For them every illusion was as real as Morgan's imagination intended. The bright orange flames engorged their lungs with smoke, but the coughs were muted as the sensory insult hit its peak.. Bright flashes of light soured from the sky signifying the surrender of the remaining pair. A silence had broken out. Morgan who had been dangling down from the pillars which held the stands, he now stood on the battle field. After months of training, it had all ended in a matter of minutes.

Everything had stopped, the ground remained untouched and the competitors remained in a state of terror as our new member was crowned rightfully victorious.

As an exhausted Morgan regained his balance, and he found the strength to raise our flag in honour of this victor. We were already celebrating wildly in the stands. Causing the foundations to quake beneath our feet as we stomped. As we celebrated the bodies of the other competitors regenerated, I smiled to see Keira remerge from the clearing smoke to hug an exhausted Morgan. Verdon made his way down to meet her, she had been on the Uppers missing list for long enough, the memory process needed to begin immediately.

Tonight we had gained a new strong member and a superb reason to gloat.

Annoyingly Hedwinn wasn't the gloating type, he simply shook hands with a furious Barasa before we left. Hedwinn's civil attitude only further angered Thomas but we brushed them off with a few overly courteous smiles. Thomas was persistent; he claimed we had asked our ancestors to place a hex on the event, in order to blind our competition.

The man was in denial - so many men lost precious land that day, not to mention the loss of pride, every moment of the last 3 days had been exhausting. I couldn't wait to return home, and we would be entering our kingdom so very triumphant. On the journey to the circus tree we raced, chanted and paraded beneath the glowing stars. Our faces reflected in the moonlight as we sprinted, behind us we left a faint trail of light and the echo of our voices. We wouldn't be returning to Balistra for many years, we would need that time just to recover!

As soon as we had arrived home, we had decided a welcome home celebration for Morgan was in order. Christina artistically and skilfully played the methodically spotless violin, she supplied a sublime soundtrack to an evening in the banquet hall. I watched the wine I had been given swishing around in the long stemmed glass, yet to take a sip. I looked up to welcome the smiling faces of Hedwinn and an equally merry Verdon. Hedwinn was tapping two empty wine glasses together, clearing his throat and glancing in Morgan's direction.

"Tonight we heard a lions roar, tonight we danced with our ancestors under the stars of Balistra. Tonight we were victorious!"

We all stamped our feet as we hailed the accomplishments of the strongest members of our team.

"Recovery will be a slow process for you my friend, but it will be well worth the effort, no matter the man, creature or immortal soul that chooses to stand against us. We will rise up with strength, with you beside us we are resilient in heart and in mind. I have the greatest honour in training and championing our newest member. Morgan Avalon!"

We all raised our glasses and repeated Hedwinn's last heartfelt words.

"Morgan Avalon!" The bewitching melody started up again. I looked over to an exhausted Morgan, barely able to stay conscious in his chair. His permanent transformation would take place in hiding tomorrow morning.

The chattering and soft harmonised music was crudely interrupted by the unexpected entrance of an animated and exuberant stranger into the room. The chamber erupted into a chorus of angry voices and violent hisses. The violin was flung against the wall as Christina was simultaneously shielded by the protective shoulder of Hedwinn.

Genevieve and Kayleigh created a body barrier between the man and I whose dark eyes matched his dark skin. Verdon and Aluma joined beside the twins to completely seclude me and Morgan from the outsider's sight. Unable to catch his breath the man fell to his knees in front the twins, Hedwinn and Christina made their way over to us with protective and menacing postures.

As they all stood to my defence my persistent heart began to stumble over itself. Hedwinn marched closer and advanced to grab the man by his filthy stained collar. Hedwinn pulled him up from his knees, his feet no longer within touching distance of the ground. Unlike the rest I was unfamiliar with the man Hedwinn was now demanding information from, I couldn't see the imposter.

Until a tear in his trousers revealed the grey mark which uncovered his identity, it was Barasa.

"How dare you enter our compound uninvited, I should exile you on principle! Give me one good reason I shouldn't banish your already pitiful existence?"

The man lifted his head from below his shoulders, his pained eyes meeting the demanding eyes of Hedwinn. With two words our opinion had changed from one of hostility to one of curiosity.

"Save Fiona!" He wimped. We were oblivious to the badly beaten woman he was protecting. As he spoke her name an ear bursting scream ripped through the halls of Avalon. I pushed passed the shield which had surrounded me and hurled myself towards the direction of the increasingly iritic cries from the woman. A red haired woman had collapsed on the marble floor which was now covered in black blood. She was bleeding profusely, her blood began pouring from her side. Her ribs were now stabbing through her pale skin. I knew in that moment Hedwinn would not orchestrate the saving of this female. She had been so kind to me on her first meeting, I wasn't about to let her die.

She wasn't one of us - Hedwinn was under no obligation to save her, I knelt down beside her as I tried to gain her consciousness. I moved her hair from her face, I gulped as the grey mark was unveiled on her forehead and continued along her skull, covered by her vibrant hair. She certainly wasn't one of us; she was not constricted to the same diet as us, she was hardly recognisable in this state. Her skin was so much like Rhena's. She was dying, her body was not as young as mine. She would not recover.

Just like Barasa she lived on both animal blood and human meat, but this wasn't worth a death sentence she was about to serve. I believed she should be given a second chance, in the hope I that could convert her to our way of life,. A I placed my hand on the woman I began to transfer some of her wounds to myself. I knew that

Hedwinn would find a way to save me. I glanced over my shoulder to see the horrified expressions of the onlookers until I collapsed onto the marble floor. I felt the liquid now pouring from my side; my orange blood drenched my clothing within a matter of seconds. The secret I was holding in, regarding my ability was no longer a secret. The fact they now knew lodged an extra pain into my side.

*****

I woke up into my overly bright bedroom, with absolutely no idea how much time had passed since the intrusion. The brash sound of an intrusive knock at my bedroom door had me dragged from the bed and within seconds. My sore quivering hand clasped onto the door handle. Reluctantly I pulled it away from its frame, without introduction Aluma who was I noticed up-close was both tall and tremendously freckled. She swivelled past me and into my rapidly changing bedroom. Once in my room Aluma began pacing slowly back and forth. Her long fingers fiddled with her collection of rings. Her fiddling drew my attention to a distorted mark, weaved between the delicate folds of wrinkles which had consumed her entire feeble body.

She was certainly the eldest member of our kind. I still can't fathom how she must feel being endlessly trapped in this life, with such a timeworn frame. Although she did have beautiful silver locks which complimented her crumpled skin. Her incessant ramblings were becoming increasingly muffled and harder to understand amongst all the murmurs. With a tap on the shoulder I carefully interrupted her; she began to calm her tone and slow her speech to a more audible rate.

"Slow down." I smiled reassuringly but her concerned expression did not budge.

"You must follow me at once, we have so much to discuss. Now that you are done with your theatrical overly dramatic acts of heroism. Honestly child what were you thinking?" Her tone was sarcastic and sharp.

Before I could respond to her criticism she instructed me to follow her down the corridor. I felt as though I was taking a long walk down the plank heading towards my judgement, how right I was. As we entered the assembly room which I had been under the impression was only used for large gatherings such as special occasions, the crowned silenced the moment I entered. Before I arrived it seemed like everyone had been taking part in what seemed to be a yelling contest, everyone was attempting to get their opinions heard – I took one of the two spare chairs around the huge oak table. A thankful looking Hedwinn emerged from his grand seat at the head of the table.

"Eva we are so very glad you have taken so well to our persistent healing rituals. But you must not keep anything such as your ability from us again. You have to grasp the potential consequences of your actions. We are very grateful you were not killed!

"In light of recent events, I'm sorry but we need you to tell us exactly what happened when you encountered Julia. We have some new intelligence which could compromise our very livelihood."

I grimaced nervously as I glanced around the seemingly growing table it was either growing or I was shirking, metaphorically of course. Never the less all the faces were eagerly staring at me; I nodded gradually, my hands clutched my knees under the table. I deliberated over where to start. When I finally found the right place, I spoke quickly - this was never a memory I relished in retelling.

"I remember slipping in and out of consciousness so you will have to forgive the holes in my memory. I was woken by the new wave of pain surged through my body in irregular short intervals. I could hear myself occasionally calling out for…"

I stopped for a moment then reassessed my thoughtless words. "The second thing I remember is the chains, as I tried to move I was met with thick steel bars. Shocking me every time any part of my body hit them. I was completely restricted. I winced repeatedly as my attempts to move failed me, every muscle in my body ached.

"The sound of the buzzing coming from the bars drowned almost everything else out. Most of all I remember the face of my elder half- sister Amelia who was in a larger less constricting cage opposite mine. I had gotten the impression Julia wasn't expect Amelia to be in my company when she grabbed me."

I watched as all the brows rose around the table as I spoke about my half-sister Amelia.

"She was the sound I had been hearing in a low repetitive whispers, she had been calling out to me. It was hard to hear anything over the noise of the cage. As soon as I gathered the strength to stay conscious, she told me she had discovered a way out of her cage. She crawled under the cage screaming as she was being shocked by the electric triggers which kept us inside the bars.

"That was the last time I saw Amelia, it wasn't long before Julia noticed she was missing. I watched her slaughter seventeen innocent and terrified people that day. She was so unbelievably humiliated and furious. Selfishly I was just glad it wasn't me she was taking her anger out on."

I stopped talking for a moment as I composed myself. The twins took my silence as an opportunity to question me.

"How the *devil* did you escape?" Genevieve and Kayleigh asked simultaneously.

"I had my mobile phone, for days I had been trying to silence its relentless buzzing in my pocket. I ignored it in fear Julia would take it from me. The moment Julia had gone to track down Amelia. I pressed the button for loudspeaker and called him back." I took a moment to smile to myself, quickly retracting it as I remembered I was the only supporter of him within these now silent walls.

"As I described the woman who had captured me everything became clear. The reason I was so weak, the reason my mouth watered as I watched Julia sleigh all those men. I knew what I had become and so did he, little did I know Julia had listened to every word of our conversation. Leering out of sight she waited for her moment to ponce once I had said too much. If I didn't comply with her demands, I wouldn't be here today. So I did everything she asked."

I bit my lip.

"Everything she asked?" Questioned an astonished and clearly repulsed Verdon. I knew I was about to reveal something I prayed I would never have to speak of again. Something disturbing and potentially damming to my character.

"Yes, Julia forced me to end the life of a man." My lips twisted uncomfortable, my hands clasped together under the table as loud gasps erupted around the room.

"I did what I was asked, but it back fired on her part, the strength it gave me was overwhelming. It allowed me to out run her. I slashed apart the bars as she hunted once more and I ran for my life."

Hedwinn stood behind me to calm my increasingly fitful state, his hands lightly gripping my tender shoulders. Hedwinn halted the others chattering, scowls were coming my way in every direction. I had broken the law in their eyes; I had committed an offence worthy of execution, Hedwinn shunned the others into silence. Maintaining that I was the victim. That without me following orders, I wouldn't have found my way home, to Avalon. With that the horrified expressions relaxed into acceptance as they couldn't find reason in which to argue against the truth in Hedwinn's word.

"Thank you." Hedwinn looking in my direction now, I smiles gratefully.

"Thank you for giving us this invaluable and intimate insight it could not have been easy for you to relive that. At least now we have a clearer understanding of why Julia has made several attempts to destroy the Circus tree's. They provide us the passageways we need to seek out new members. She had destroyed 5 of the portals already; she and her father are threatening to end our connection to the Uppers world. She knows without it we couldn't function, Julia knows she would be cutting you off from ever returning home. Preventing you telling anyone of how you were able to humiliate and mock her attempt to make you her protégé. The Balistra battles at which she was humiliated would be no more.

"Eva the reason Barasa came to us was because Magnus and Julia had attempted to take over their tribe with violence. They're lucky to be alive along with yourself, the pair are attempting to take leadership of other covens by force. We know who the next target is, but we also know Julia and Magnus were not alone. The two have created an almighty following of many stray confused vampires.

"We are all going to need to pull together, we have something they don't sure she may now match us as far as numbers are concerned. Let us not forget that she has inherited her father's cowardice amongst many frightful things. Her new members will in time see her weaknesses and will no longer be blinded by undeserved loyalty. Let us be the ones to open their eyes."

My breath quickened with astonishment as a rush of excitement washed over me. A rightful need for justice took over every feeling of hesitation I had, about what was likely to be a murderous spree.

"How is it that they are able to change so many people without causing a riot?" My hands wavering with both desperation and a new enthusiasm for the fight.

"When you change a person into being one of our kind, you do not just determine which mark they will bare.

You also give them a piece of who you are. Julia possess great stealth and an ability to sneak under the defences built up to protect her.

"You have clearly inherited some of her abilities and so have the others she is converting. Giving the stray vampires no option but to join her is against the laws of Avalon. You Eva are the only one who could end her existence alone, something which many of us have failed to do in the distant past. In the conversation she overheard when you were in captivity, she has recognised that you have close relatives beyond Avalon. They could be in danger if we do not put an end to her reign. This changes everything, we have no choice but to destroy Julia, this will not be easy Eva but if you are willing, you will not be asked to take on such a tremendous task alone."

My stomach churned, Julia was on an unstoppable mission to cut off every connection we had to the rest of the world, and to the other vampires. It was as if a light bulb had turned on above my head and suddenly I blurted out.

"What about the other vampires - the Phethlim tribe for example? After all, I saved his mate, Fiona right? If anything they owe us. Julia did this to her then who knows who is next on her list. Those vampires who wander alone still utilise our land, if that want that right to remain, they should be given the option to join us." I could feel the tension mounting in the hostel room, never had all 3 covens come together in aid of one another.

"Think about it, she is looking for protégés to destroy each of the kingdom, so she can rule over every breed including the Uppers. No more fighting for territory - she and Magnus are not going to stop until they have power and control over Avalon. If they can close our portals and do what she did to Fiona. Think about what her protégés can achieve within other vampire circles? She could potentially ruin many communities.

"Certainly, with this knowledge we can come together as one unit, to fight against her and her team of stray vampires she has collected! I cannot defeat her alone and the others she is assembling. Neither can just one collection of us. Feeding differences aside, let us fight together."

Hedwinn held a thoughtful expression which reflected that of every other member around the table. A unanimous nod took a turn around the table. Fiona and Barasa were going to be the first of many to take our side in this; it was time to change our words into long overdue actions.

# 6. BRAVERY, CHECK!

I had been under the incorrect presumption that time only sped up when you were enjoying yourself, so I couldn't understand why the days leading up to the confrontation flew by so quickly. It was as if time itself was becoming impatient for the combat. The intervals within which I was given time to rest was readily decreasing, but I don't think any of us minded the exhaustion too much. I have always thought that if something doesn't require you to throw one hundred per cent of yourself into them - they are probably not worth fighting for.

Although the hours of taking on advice and learning techniques were gruelling, we all shared one united understanding of the end value. We knew with certainty everyone would have to be in the very best shape to conquer their potential. We needed to be at our strongest both collectively and individually, so of course I offered my services to the cause. Every third day I would help to heal another member of the clan, the consequences of which were mostly small. I was able to heal faster than the others with my being the youngest. For me it felt like respite was not an option. After all I had set this train into motion I was the trigger that had ultimately shot Julia into action.

Before any of us knew it the kingdom was alive with activity, the new faces of the other clans had begun arriving in waves over the duration of ten days. We were completely outnumbered by the many members who had honourably decided join the cause. I have to admit our guests made me nervous and I wasn't the only one. Aluma was particularly unwilling to exchange pleasantries with those who she still bared grudges with. She stubbornly refused to put aside the fundamental differences between us and *them*.

Our diets would always provide a wedge between any bonds we were trying build. Luckily we would never allow it to take focus from our joint hatred of Julia and Magnus. Feeding and breeding rituals was at the root of relentless tensions between the clans; the time of collaboration could no longer be minimal.

Trying to maintain my strength was a major priority. We were all going to compete against beings who had the pleasure of feeding on the lavishly nutritious flesh, of human beings. In our clan I was the only one with any experience of what level feeding on human flesh could excel you to, and it terrified me. Thankfully our guests came baring gifts and extra supplies, in addition to their talents and numbers that is.

An enormous horde of Crazors, one of the many creatures who breed close to a circus tree patches, which had brought the tribes to our abode. They arrived via one of the very few pathways still available, thank goodness for that. I felt so barbaric eating with my hands during meal times.

The Crazors were the closest meat we could get to match the nutrition you would find in human meat and it was delicious. After a mouth-watering feast I was able to help or heal anyone who needed it. Mercifully the only injuries sustained seemed to be the occasional sprain or broken bone.

Ever since we had declared war on Julia and Magnus, Hedwinn was on constant full alert. I had never seen him like this, I laughed in conversations with Cornelius; we were both convinced Hedwinn was at least part machine. It was the only explanation as to how he was able to maintain such a constant schedule of errands. I have no idea where he was finding the strength from, constantly running inventories and accompanying Verdon on trips the portals.

Every time he would return his face would reflect the outcome, let's just say the times he would return with a smile on his face was becoming increasingly rare. Julia was closing us in one portal at a time - soon we would have no way out, she was forcing us to mobilise that bit faster.

Within a month I had healed everyone from each tribe of their long term and more recently acquired injuries. Everyone including Hedwinn, who is no longer subjected to his focus splitting headaches to which he had long endured. I even managed to heal Verdon of a fractured rib which he had sustained during a routine check of a destroyed portal.

To be honest I was exhausted, I prayed that neither Hedwinn nor Verdon would return with any serious injuries for both our sakes. I don't think I can take another injury. I haven't had enough down time to heal from my previously inherited wounds.

When I was lucky enough to catch a moment of sleep I was bombarded with dreams. The dreams in which I was allowed to visualise Tyler one more time were a blessing, at least they used to be. One evening when the hand on the silver antique cloak situated on my dresser hit 4am, I fell into another dream. This time his face was one of fear.

I couldn't believe he was afraid to be near me, as I fought my way through the sea of nettles to reach him but he continued backing away. Until he spotted my injuries that is, his left hand examined my fractured rib with fury.

In his eyes I was practically committing suicide by deliberately getting myself injured. For a purpose which he believed didn't bared the weight of my actions. He never got the chance to verbally scold me. I woke abruptly as a bolt of lightening shot diagonally through the entire length of my room. The strike smashed the only photograph I had of Tyler which had previously stood proudly on my wooden cabinet bedside my bed - the picture was irreversibly obliterated.

As I jumped out of bed my bare feet were met with freezing cold ankle deep water. I watched my breath disintegrate into the ice cold air. Heavy thick droplets of rain soaked my clothes and exposed areas of skin. The rain added to the water which sloshed irritatingly around my feet.

Another horrendous bolt of lightning struck the headboard of my bed. Collapsing it into shreds of wooden pieces, I ran to the door to escape the living nightmare.

As I dried my now soaking feet with a cotton towel I had found hidden within a cabinet outside my black bedroom door. I headed to the one place within Avalon that wasn't inhabited with the other covens - Cornelius' room.

I now knew the path to his door like the back of my hand. I walked passed Hedwinn's quarters when the sound of voices drew me to a holt. Both Hedwinn and Genevieve were talking with unusually hushed tones in the conference suite, which I had never seen being used before. The door was conveniently open just enough for me to hear what they were saying. Although it was never my intention to listen for as long as I did. I never could control my ignorant curiosity.

"The walls are closing in and time is running out Hedwinn. I need to know we are getting involved in this war for the right reasons. I don't want to throw my sister into a war in which she may be..."

A considerably frightened and vulnerable Genevieve sighed heavily. "She is the only person I have left after our mother, after Orlando..."

Hedwinn interjected to reassure her concerns. "We have every member behind us this time, we have the upper hand. I can guarantee above all else that I will go to great lengths to ensure the safety of you and your sister. I give you my word Genevieve."

I smiled at Hedwinn's natural ability to so easily comfort her, he was such a tremendous father figure to the clan, to us all he was so much more than just a leader he was a treasured friend.

As I stepped backwards my footsteps were detected by an always alert Hedwinn who ushered me into the room with a disappointed look on his face.

"Do you make a habit of listening into other individuals conversations?" Questioned a furious Genevieve. The moment I entered the room, I knew she was never one to show her vulnerable side. She feared it would reveal she had weaknesses beyond her control. She never wanted to be seen as anything other than a strong individual. She hated the idea that the covens view of her could be compromised. The worries she carried would always be in vain, Genevieve and her sister are still one of the fiercest female duo's I know.

"No, of course not I'm sorry but if I could, I would go up against Julia myself truly I would. But I doubt I could achieve anything without your help. Please don't give up on this Genevieve. We have come so far, please." Genevieve looked at me with a defeated expression and then took a seat in a dark leather chair beside the blazing fire. She offered me a seat in the chair opposite, I took it with trepidation.

I leaned forward as she began to speak, her eye contact was constantly diverted from mine. I instinctively knew that what she was about to tell me was making her highly uncomfortable.

"Eva, until you have lost a parent you will never truly understand the pain and repercussions of what I am about to tell you. Hedwinn has informed me that you are aware that this isn't the first time we have come up against Julia and her wicked father. We have tried relentlessly to both reason with and prevent, their incessant hunger for leadership and control. We have always known they would only be patient for so long.

"The devastating battle at Orlando was no different, Julia had just left us to join her father Magnus in his quest to create a kingdom of his own.

"He was never happy with the biological hand he was dealt by his ancestors. He like most of us, would have to wait in line for his chance to rule Avalon. For many millenniums, this was the agreement made by our founders. So long as we have a strong standing son of Avalon on the thrown, he cannot be replaced. This will remain until he can no longer perform the duties required to serve our kind.

"Once the pure line of Avalon is no more only then can a new family take on the role, Verdon, my sister and I were not part of the Avalon blood line. The oath we took has forged the gap between our genetics, Julia and Magnus refused this oath.

"Julia and Magnus Atum, will have to wait until each of us has served our time. Magnus is not a patient creature. He simply doesn't agree with the Triquil philosophy of equality. And our disliking to the idea of one superior leader whom wishes to exploit the other coven members. He would use us as pawns and potential sacrifices if necessary. The man is barbaric.

"We all knew Julia's departure was inevitable and worse still, she knew what we were capable of both individually and collectively. She has extensive knowledge of our capabilities and our techniques. I suppose in reflection we were doomed from the very beginning. She and Magnus ambushed us, if it wasn't for Hedwinn I wouldn't be sat here today. The members who were changed at an older age were targeted first. One of which was my mother Mrs Callista Jayne Avalon, she would have been the next in line to take over from Magnus." Her words becoming increasingly fractured as she spoke her mother's name.

"Julia herself shocked my mother's heart in front of my eyes, the same shock of electricity you used to heal my scar. She cracked my mother's chest and traumatised her heart with one electric touch." My mouth hung open in sheer terror, in that instance it all became brutally, terrifyingly and inescapably real.

Her words were that of torment, I instantly questioned whether or not I was doing the right thing All of this could be avoided, if I handed myself over. If I gave in to Julia's demands Avalon wouldn't be threatened.

If Julia and Magnus could find another way to be unbeatably victorious and powerful, then all this would go away. I knew that all Julia and Magnus ultimately wanted was to train the youngest ever turned Triquil member. This could have brought them glory equal to running a coven, without all the mandatory duties. The guilt I felt was rupturing inside my stomach; I clutched my waist tight as Genevieve composed herself enough to speak again.

"Hedwinn has just stressed the differences in the circumstances previously. We did not have half the resources we currently have, nor half the man power. The strength you have given us is an significant advantage. This time we will be the ones with the surprise element. Both sister and I have more of a motive to end her life than we ever had before you can count us in."

I nodded with gratitude. "Thank you Genevieve, truly." We both met each other for a hug I felt I wasn't the only one who needed it at this moment. I smiled faintly as my stomach continued churning. I watched them both leave the room and my desire to see Cornelius had wilted. I couldn't allow for any more timewasting.

My responsibilities were mounting.

As I opened the door, all of my furniture had vanished. There was nothing left other than the floor boards on which I sat down. Allowing my back to lean against the closed bedroom door. I rested my chin on my knees completely deflated. Everything had suddenly became clear, I really didn't deserve any of my previous luxuries. Genevieve's solemn words had sunk deep and with them, the challenge ahead had been put into a very unpleasant perspective.

I put my inability to sleep to good use and began telling myself things needed to change. Within the blink of an eye my bedroom was transformed into every bodybuilders dream. The transformation included a treadmill, several punch bags hung from the ceiling, benches, humongous weights. For additional motivation the walls were covered in a mirage of Julia's face. Her eyes staring at me from every direction.

As I strapped on my newly acquired boxing gloves around my wrists, it wasn't long until I had beads of sweat were forming around my brows. My hands were moving faster than my eyes could keep up with.

The harder I pushed myself the quicker I became, rocketing around the room so fast I was unable to catch my reflection in the mirror. I was able to kick the bag which hung from the clouds. I hit it so forcefully it smashed into the wall, forcing it free of the rope holding it in place. Using my hands I shielded my face as bricks imploded from the wall. The moment I pulled my arms back, the wall began repairing itself as though never dismantled.

I grinned contently and began again.

# 7. HAPPY BIRTHDAY

## March 14th 2014

As I stretched out my well rested limbs, I squeezed my fingertips and toes in slow rhythmic motions. I opened my eyes and I smirked with delight. My bedroom was heavily decorated with mammoth bright purple balloons, they hovered beside beautiful lilac celebratory banners. The beautiful sun beamed through the balloons creating a purple mirage. The colours spanning along my part of building, in various illuminating shades.

I grinned as my favourite colour danced along my chamber; although I wasn't technically aging today it was a celebration of the last year, and what was to come. I thought of it not as a coming of age celebration but more of a coming to life commemoration. We only had two full weeks until the point of no return would come along, so I was going to make the very most of today if nothing else.

As I stepped from beneath my decorative covers, I ran my hands down my sides. I was made conscious of extra weight and soft fabric clinging to my body. As I looked down I was stunned by a beautiful heavy dress which flowed elegantly from my below my arms to my feet, cleverly hidden by the two foot train.

As I spun around in my new dress I was overwhelmed with a rush of endorphins, they fuelled my every smile. Stopping mid swirl as my attention was drawn to my door which displayed a red flashing arrow. Opening it expectantly I glanced down the corridor. My rested eyes widened as I was startled by a series of similar arrows, all pointing towards the end of the hallway.

Following them with curiosity, the final pointer led me towards the breakfast room. As I stepped inside I was met with an overpowering combination of scents. I deciphered the cooking of Crazors and the sweet smell of ripe strawberries. After I had taken a seat at the large oak table one by one the chairs around the counter became host to different members of our clan both new and old. I smiled as Genevieve and Kayleigh entered first, hugging me tightly and complimenting my unusually desirable attire.

"Thank you so much everyone!" Kayleigh dangled a key a silver key in front of her face, as I examined the key. I raised my confused plucked brow.

"What is this for?" I asked as they both gracefully took their seats. Doors in Avalon were about as redundant as money, what is there here that I am yet to unlock? With humble gratitude I placed the key onto the small delicate gold chain of my pendant..

"This key opens any and every slot you put it into. So you can think of it as a belated homecoming gift also." Stated a proud Kayleigh. "Wow, I don't know what to say, thank you so much, it's great. It's better than any gift I could have thought up, impressive." I grinned as I watched the twins cutting up the impressive spread of cooked Crazors. Along with condiments, the table was overflowing with wonderful food.

I glanced to the door as I heard the forthcoming echo of voices and footsteps from the corridor behind me. Before I knew it the table was full with guests from the Phelium and Gohinease covens.

"**Happy Birthday!**" Bellowed the thrilled crowed, it was rare that everyone came together especially around something as controversial as the dinner table.

I couldn't help but notice the wealth of faces around me were all so distinctive. I was always surrounded by beautiful people, for once the atmosphere was so pure. I watched in delight as the covens made small talk between one another. Including Verdon and Kaylum the second male was the one member from the Phethlim tribe.

Kaylum had the fairest slicked back hair of any male I'd ever met, his thin lips, thin eyebrows, high cheek bones and a rounded chin made him undeniably distinguished. Admirably he made the decision to abandon his coven and convert to our ways, in order to fight beside us. He was incredibly sociable and I had found him to be such a joker. He was previously acting as messenger for his tribe it gave Verdon and him a great deal to talk about. It was great to see him bonding so naturally. It gave me hope for some of the more reluctant elder members of our coven.

Another brave man had also donated himself to the cause, Sam Stewart was so easily fitting into the fabric of our life. Sam had come to us from the Phethlim coven. He like Morgan earned his place in this life, his battle skills were certainly a blessing. As he sat diagonal from me I could see his trim facial hair partially hidden by his high polo neck jumper. His veiny hands clenched around the bones of a Crazor as he began speaking with a still weak Morgan. Sam, in his late thirties, was certainly the muscle of the group. Although he didn't like to make a fuss of his strengths, they were outstanding. Not to mention completely immortal.

It was extremely disappointing that no women had come forward to fight with us. Many female figures didn't bare the same opportunities as men, in other misogynous covens. Verdon and Kaylum took up their seats opposite me.

Verdon placed a white sealed card on the table, he pushed it flat across the table. I secretively picked up the card and with a glance and a few words, Verdon requested I open it later. I smiled and whispered. "Thank you."

I anxiously placed the letter on my lap, the weight of it growing heavier with each passing minute; I now knew what money felt like to a child, burning a hole in the adolescence pocket. As I looked around the room with a different perspective, I noticed we were still missing a pinnacle member of the group. Even with my swarm of friends and family around me, all 9 of them I still missed the other 2.

The swarm included our Aluma, the twins, Barasa, Fiona, Morgan, the 2 messengers and Sam. Hedwinn and Christina's absence was still felt. Without them we were like a well-oiled machine, minus the heart that kept us all going. Hedwinn had been spending a lot of time rebuilding Morgan's strength. Enough so he could at least leave his quarters to gather food; I hadn't really seen much of them since the battle, I was just glad that Morgan was now at least able to make it to the table.

My attention was diverted as a grinning Fiona and her gradually reforming mate Barasa handed me a tall glass. Filled to the brim with a frosted cool purple smoothly, as a small peace offering. Placing the glass to my nose I tried to pick out the blend.

"Blueberries, cranberries, dragon fruit and…" I struggled to pick out the last ingredient, I sniffed again. **"Crazors blood!"**

Informed a politely smug Barasa, he was trying hard to build up bridges had dug such a deep grave for himself. That man could move the heavens and either of the earths and he would barely scratch the surface. But my god he was trying - I had to give him that.

"You guys, considering you only eat Crazors and human meat, I am impressed at you knowledge of other natural resourceful ingredients." I took a sip and hummed as the taste set alight my previously numbed taste buds.

"That's incredible." As I sipped on my new favourite beverage, Barasa's vintage swade brown watch caught my attention. Magnificently it reflected from the sunlight bursting from above, constantly catching my eye.

My observation had not been ignored. Barasa followed my gaze back from his wrist until he was looking at me directly in the eye.

"It belonged to an old friend of mine, from the Upper level." I gulped; wiping my mouth on a peach napkin. We all knew that Barasa's kind didn't keep 'friends' on the Upper ground. I instantly knew he must have taken it from one of his victims. The small delicate pointers on the watch weren't moving, stuck on midnight. I arched my brow with intrigue.

"I could fix it if you'd like?" I said as Barasa grinned to an unusually quiet and captivated audience.

"It's broken for a purpose, you see it's almost an insider's joke regarding time. Those on the level above are so governed by time. They live, eat and sleep by what the counters indicate.

Upper are so restricted by time converting into months and eventually years. To them they also have so many decades before they reach their expiration date. We on the other hand, do not suffer the same limitations, much to my amusement." I was stunned by his revelry, his understanding of the Uppers existence kept me thinking. I hated the fact that he was ultimately correct.

The noise in the room picked up as finally Hedwinn and Christina entered the room. In seconds our bodies we were beating loud and proud once more. I quickly put down my glass and stood up to greet him as his wife Christina took her seat.

Christina, was most recognisable because of her unconventional features, in many ways I regarded her as everything I could ever want to be and more. When her eyes weren't black with hunger which wasn't very often. She had the most prominent breathtakingly stunning red eyes.

In a previously male dominated metropolis she had managed to nurture the twins and she had even given Fiona a few lessons in independence. Out of all the women from whom Hedwinn could have chosen as a mate, he plucked her fifty decades ago.

Another defining feature she possessed was her white and black mark which was placed along the nape of her neck. To any individual not in the know, you'd think she'd naively allowed tattoo artists to have free rain over her skin.

However, unlike some of the others around the table she wore her marking with great pride. In her mind it was grander and more meaningful than any ring Hedwinn could conjure for her. She wore it as a symbol of her choice. She was a wonderer when Hedwinn and Verdon came across her on a visit to a southern tribe; she hadn't technically been claimed by any other tribe.

She found substance on feeding on the dead carcass of various animals. At the time she had been introduces to a member of the Phethlim tribe. But she was very much swayed by the magnetic charms of the current Mr Avalon himself.

In my eyes she had become an inspirational matriarch not only to me but the other women beside me. Marvellously she would often supply the music accompaniments to our evening assemblies with her violin. She would entertain us with harrowing tales from her former life. We often discussed the two ways you come into this existence, either you are bitten by an existing vampire. Or the less likely route is that you are born into a half-bred family.

Christina had been bitten by a full human hunting vampire. Unlike the rest of our coven she suffered chronic hunger pains that not even I could take away. Despite my repetitive best efforts. Unlike any of ours, her decision to stick with Hedwinn in spite of her needs was a courageous one.

"Happy Birthday Eva, I apologise for my being late, I had to acquire your gift." Hedwinn smiled brightly and then handed me a square shaped gift box wrapped in reflective silver paper. The beautifully decorated present was complete with a purple ribbon tied delicately at the centre.

As I tore open the wrapping paper, saving the bow, I arched my brow. "A calendar?" I hugged Hedwinn and Christina with a smile. "Thank you both so much." As I flicked through the calendar, I noticed it didn't bare any pictures to represent each month. Across the other side of the room I heard Barasa huffing. I wasn't going to allow him to ruin the thoughtful gift.

"Try it out." He requested with a hint of sarcasm to his tone.

"What do you mean?" Hedwinn laid out the calendar on the solid oak kitchen dining table. In a couple of seconds I noticed the calendar didn't bare any dates at all, today was March 22nd, 2014. Hedwinn pointed to a blank square on the calendar.

"Touch it." I bit my lip and nodded as I placed my finger to yesterday's date, suddenly I could see myself training in my room the previous day. In calendars display window above the list of days within the week. As I pulled back my hand the image froze into the frame.

"Wow Hedwinn, I love it!" As I flicked back I thought about my birthday last year, placing my finger in the square which attracted me most. I watched myself in my mind's eye blowing out candles on my nineteenth birthday cake. This time last year with my mortal family. As I pulled back the image within the square froze into one of the cake, I smiled gratefully to Hedwinn and Christina.

"You have many memories to make for the coming year, be sure to make them good ones Eva." I hugged him again appreciatively. "Without a doubt!"

As I looked at the photograph of the birthday cake, purple frosting with sickly sweet blue writing icing, I started to feel homesick for time spent with my Upper family. Before I had left my Uppers home my sister had just gotten engaged to Mathew. My mom had just given them permission to move in, just until they could afford their own place. I knew the house would be very crowded. I closed the booklet.

I chewed my lip before finally managing to get Verdon's attention. Looking over to him I suggestively nudged my head towards the door luckily without the knowledge of the others. I rose from my chair and headed towards the corridor, Verdon followed behind me. Closing the door behind us, I paced back and forth as I probed him with all my questions.

"Did you see him? Is he alright? Does he hate me? Did you talk?" Verdon shook his head at my questions patiently answering them one by one. I wanted so badly to probe his brain. I was in desperate need of answers, I wished I could see every moment. The only thing I had asked for my birthday this year was for Verdon to retrieve a letter for me from Tyler.

"We didn't exchange pleasantries; he seems to be handling things rather well." I nodded.

"Did you see him with anyone?" I didn't exactly relish the idea of Tyler confiding in another woman. But I knew it was a better alternative to him containing his anger and resentment towards me.

"He was with his brothers at his current residence." I took a breath, at least that's one worry I could put to bed. "Thank you Verdon, for doing this, it means a lot."

Verdon took a moment to reply. "I hope it contains everything you wish it to, if not. Don't dwell on the unobtainable." I grimaced.

As we both walked back into the room I was glad to see our absence had gone unnoticed, and even if the others had noticed our disappearance no one questioned it. We both took our seats back around the buzzing table to complete our stunning meals.

Once I had eaten what I knew would be an acceptable amount, I needed some time to myself. Somewhere I wouldn't be disturbed. After hugging everyone I headed off to see Cornelius. Taking with me my precious gifts to explore them privately.

As much as part of me wanted to read the letter, another part of me was happy to stay blissfully in denial for a few more days. In my pool of denial I could pretend no time had passed, I could make-believe that Tyler still loved me, I wasn't ready to let that illusion go.

Instead I sat flicking through the pages of my new photographic diary, I kept glancing up at Cornelius. His never changing complexion was looking down on me, as I spoke. "Cornelius, if you could get out of here, be real for just one day sort of a Cinderella deal - what would you do with your time and boundless freedom?"

He looked back to me, pausing for a few seconds till he conjured up an answer. I counted the shattering sound of his blinks as he paused in thought...10, 11, 12, 13...

"As you know, my only points of reference in regards to what is outside these walls is derived from what you have experienced. If I was given no other option but to choose I suppose I would like to just be in the company of the people I love. And those who appreciate the gesture. I can't imagine what having such a strong emotion for another being must feel like."

I smiled brightly. "It is not so terrible I suppose, although I do think you're forgetting my little encounter with Edmund Riviera." He chuckled with me as I flicked through the pages to June, placing my finger over the 17th June, 2013. Closing my eyes to allow myself to be completely amerced by the scenery of the illusive pre-Tyler memory.

The doorbell rang; I was finding it difficult to pull myself out of my own troublesome thoughts. Even just for long enough to concentrate on doing the simple task of opening the door, to greet Edmund.

I took the slow walk downstairs, straightened out my dress, and flung my hair over my shoulder, still warm from Amelia's hair straighteners. She insisted that having wavy hair during the date would show a lack of preplanning on my part. Before I opened the white door, I could see him waiting behind the stained glass, I sighed.

At this point in my life, I had found a new reason to be grateful. Over the years I'd had so much practice at perfecting my multitude of disguises. Whether it was disguising feelings for Tyler for as long as I did, or concealing my life's problems from my Upper family.

As soon as I pulled back the door I smiled to Edmund as his eyes widened, I instinctively bit my lip. I was a complete bag of potentially damaging nervous. My outfit wasn't exactly what he or anyone else would expect to see me in, not even close to my usual get-up.

He took my hand in his and kissed my gold ring accidentally, I knew he had been aiming for the back of my hand. It looked like I wasn't the only being gagged by the bag of 'oh so' excellent nerves; we laughed it off as he led me to his brand new sports car.

Whilst putting on my seatbelt, I looked over my shoulder to my mini cooper parked so unassuming in the drive way. Damn I miss that car.

Suddenly I was pulled out of the memory, I began taking in breathes, shook my head and looked back at Cornelius.

"Human memories, they can be so difficult to connect with sometimes."

Cornelius smiled at me and simply said. "You can do it." With that I pushed myself back into the memory with the sound of Edmunds voice. "So, where we headed Eva?"

He said whilst flashing a cavalier smile my way. "Anywhere, I don't mind." I was being honest with him, I didn't mind. I just needed this diversion, no matter the destination.

Much to my disappointment this seemingly fool proof distraction wasn't exactly working. As we drove toward one of the few decent restaurants in town, my mind was fast becoming a replica of the dynamics of a complicated jigsaw. The only pieces obediently fitting into the correct places were the ones concerning Tyler.

Everything else just didn't make sense; they didn't fit not even close. Each jagged edge set me back even further. It was as though he was living in another world - now look how things have turned out.

As we arrived at the restaurant he opened my car door again. He helped me out by taking my hand gently, with more confidence and conviction in his demeanour. As we stepped inside the busy dinner room hand in hand, I was overwhelmed by the sheer quantity of people in the restaurant.

The middle aged male waiter smiled towards Edmund, he began gesturing toward a table which Edmund must have pre-booked. Unfortunately beside the was my old school tutor, the awkwardness level was almost palpable. The small intimate table already had a bottle of 2001 Champagne in the centre, contained in a cylinder of ice. I tried to force my eyes not to roll at this point. I really didn't need this whole charade complete with overly pretentious props.

My mind constantly flashing back to when I saw Tyler earlier in the day; I didn't want anything else then to be with him in so many different capacities. In a single instant with Tyler a connection was planted so effortlessly. I had been drawn to him indefinitely without any charade needing to be put in place to create a spark. Nothing remotely forced like this seemed to be.

I smirked at the thought as I sat down on the chair, the waiter had pulled out for me. Quickly I began scanning the menu aimlessly. The painful truth was dawning on me minute by agonising minute. I was slowly finding out that Edmund wasn't the only one who was putting on an act tonight. I was also performing, badly. This entire imitation of happiness was tiresome, I was tired of trying to move on from someone I had no desire to move on from. It was too late to back out now. Try as I did, I couldn't think of a way to speed this process up without:

a) hurting Edmunds feelings

b) looking like a fool

There was no middle ground. So I had to sit in a complete state of numbness eating opposite Edmund, who was clearly enjoying this more than I was.

"Eva? You look very lovely this evening." His eyes once more glimmered over my outfit, scanning every speckle of my visible skin that was on show. He acted as though I were already his.

"Thanks, it's not one of my favourite outfits." I laughed lightly as he greedily polished his plate of spaghetti. He had finished before I had scraped the sides of mine. With my mouth still full he stroked my cheek, claiming I had a spot of sauce lingering on my face.

I never was a sloppy eater.

I vaguely remember a short man lingering around our table holding a bouquet of single stemmed red roses in his hand. He began wandering between the tables, selling them I assumed. He was also loitering around the groups of happy couples trying to entice someone in the reasonably packed restaurant to purchase them. As soon as my eyes were back on Edmund he was gesturing to the man. My face became awash with an embarrassingly bright red.

"One for the lady if you don't mind."

Edmund took money from his leather wallet and handed it to him. He smiled with a slight smirk which further fuelled my embarrassment.

"Oh thank you Edmund that's very thoughtful of you." I took the rose in my hand and kissed Edmund on the cheek. But still I felt nothing not even a flicker of interest, no desire for anything more. Nothing.

The table was being cleared and the same fair-haired waiter who firstly greeted us then asked. "Is there anything else? Dessert menu perhaps?"

My response was immediate "No thank you, I couldn't take another mouthful."

"She's sweet enough." Edmund chuckled to himself as he folded his napkin in his hands, the waiter swiftly moved on. I wanted this to be over. I was already mentally dating someone who at the time barely knew I was interested.

As I pulled back my hand from the calendar thus removing myself from the memory, I looked to Cornelius with a weary smile.

"Now, let me ask you again, what would you do with freedom if you were given it?" Cornelius chuckled. "Maybe not Edmund, I think you know who I was referring too." I laughed and nodded respectfully.

# 8. MY UPPER FAMILY

From the outside Avalon had everything you could ever ask for and more, but the beautiful walls did not house beautiful young souls. The one thing Avalon didn't have was a nursery full of children. We never did hear the pitter patter of tiny feet against the marble floors, in fact aged 19 I was the youngest member of our coven in history. As far as I knew, it was still possible to conceive in this half human existence. I don't mean to say it would be an easy thing to achieve but certainly not impossible.

Unlike the full bred covens Triquils did not need to recruit Uppers to take the place of withering vampires. We could procreate. I had been informed Avalon had previously been one of the safest places, that was before Magnus and Julie became out of control. We possessed some of the best genetic and coveted genetic material for a member of our kind. Julia and Magnus had robbed us in more ways than one. I had asked our eldest member Aluma why Avalon was no longer host to chubby faces and tiny toes. She had explained that views were very much spilt on the matter. She also stated to me that I was indeed the youngest person, ever person to step foot on the floors of Avalon.

I am only 19 I protested, she shook her head with dwindling patients and informed me of something we both knew to be true. I had been much younger than 19 when I fell to the floors here.

For a moment I reminisced my much earlier conversations with Hedwinn. I enquired as to how it was possible for the coven to have predicted that I would one day encounter the wrath of Julia. How did Hedwinn know to be at the right place at the right time. In order to find me? Surely it was no coincidence. Hedwinn smiled brightly and told me that the reason they knew I would one day be a member of this elite group. The information was all derived from the psychic musings of Harpitunia.

Harpitunia was the combined craftsmanship of several elders hard work through the centuries, she became more than a material position. The harp was brought to life by the power of a very wise elder. From the moment she was crafted she became a living insightful instrument.

I was in awe as Hedwinn described in detail Harpitunia's remarkable hand constructed structure. Strings constructed to curve in order to create a working vocabulary. They vibrated to allow words and phrases to be formed. Its frame created from the seedlings and bark of various precious Circus trees.

I frantically demanded he take me to the Harp. I growled at initial lack of pre thinking - what if it could tell me if the impending battle was already lost?

It could tell us Magnus' and Julia's precise location, we could plan the perfect ambush greater than the one the pair were hatching, it could give us the upper hand. As I tripped over my words the elderly Aluma hastily interrupted mine and Hedwinn's conversation. Informing me that Harpitunia had been destroyed by Magnus. Aluma told me that before Magnus left for the last time, in a fit of rage he destroyed the harp. After it confirmed he would have to wait many millenniums to finally become a candidate to rule over Avalon and its people. The hierarchy never sat right with him.

I exhaled heavily. Harpitunia was one of the many things we weren't going to be able to utilise, in order to defeat the duo. Morgan was also still unable to attend the battle, much to his disappointment. He wanted so desperately to further prove his loyalty to show what he could do without the rules and restrictions of Balistra. But the battle had taken so much of his energy out that without rest he would surely be slaughtered.

The elder woman later told me that the second last prediction which Harpitunia had made was the exact date and location of where Hedwinn would find me, oh how marvellous she was and could have continued to be.

Verdon, Hedwinn and the twins had all taken several shifts to protect the last remaining Circus trees; luckily for me no one had sustained any injuries. In a way, I couldn't help but see the unspoken side to the lack of attacks. I knew that if Magnus and Julia were not attacking the trees then they were more than likely plotting, recruiting or mobilising. I did what I could to contribute.

For the most part my involvement included me taking cooking lessons from Fiona and Aluma, at least I wasn't entirely useless. Thankfully I was a fast learner and only burnt a couple of Crazors throughout the interesting learning process. Along with cooking I was also managing the entire covens workout schedule, I was becoming as relentless as those preparing to attack us.

After a little while I was starting to forget what my room looked like without my extensive collection of exercise equipment. Or what my body felt like without the various aches and pains. But I knew eventually the hard work would all pay off. Of course if I wasn't exercising, sleeping or cooking I was familiarising myself with the different machinery we would need to defeat Julia and Magnus.

I had to be able to confidently and skilfully use the equipment to end the malicious lives of the pair. We knew the only way to defeat them was to divide and conquer. Separating them however wasn't going to be an easy task. One of the many weapons I was training to use was the deadly Fredishdine whip.

The whip is as sharp as shark's teeth and just as fatal. With one strike, your torso would be split in two it was able to slash through even the most durable of skins.

Hedwinn was training me on using all manner of artilleries, as I watched the twins training which had certainly given me a lot to emulate; I couldn't help but notice how elegant and fierce they both were. The two were effortlessly in sync with one another. Whilst observing them I thought about how I would hate to be on the receiving end of their fury.

With everything that was happening I barely had time to think about the letter I requested for my birthday. The one that I knew contained the concerned musings of Tyler. Reading it could prove that I really was gluten for punishment, looking back it really was inevitable that his words would be of deep contempt. It was time to leave my warm pool of denial and, step out into the bitterly cold winds of his rejection.

The letter had my name scribbled on the front in his messy hand writing, as I ran my finger over it I could feel the indentation into the envelope. Sat on the cycle trainer I began to peddle as I toyed with the letters seal reluctantly, with bravery I finally tore it open. Unfolding the letter I instantly began reading his words - luckily the handwriting inside was less erratic.

Eva please come home, I need you and Amelia needs you. She and Mathew are having a child you're going to be an aunt. This has been out of control for too long now. I'll give you until one week after your birthday. I will be waiting at the park at midnight alone. You know which one I mean, if you're not there I will know you have made the wrong choice.

I never thought there would be anything that could overpower our relationship but this isn't about us it's about your safety. If you won't put yourself first then you leave me no choice, I will come for you.

You can't let Julia determine your fate, this is where you belong - this is your home.

Please don't make me come for you.

I will leave no living being of your kind or mine unquestioned as to your whereabouts.

March 21st Eva, be there.

At the end of the letter he hadn't signed his name or even said goodbye, no kisses, no 'love you'.

I fell back from the siting upright as the chair transformed back into a bed. Not one I recognised right away. The 4 walls had transformed again, not with my mood, but to something I desired. Tyler's room; well as I could remember it. The layout was exactly the same but there was still some dark patches, especially in pictures of his family.

Trying to recreate his room from memory was an impossible task, I only wished the rooms capabilities stretched beyond the fabrication of the walls. I wanted Tyler. I was however able to see his assortment of sketches on display. He was so talented - we had decided to keep the images over at his place, until we could afford to have them framed.

Other than the occasional lunch date, I hadn't been in his house very often throughout our 3 year relationship. I had only been in his room a few times; he was always at my place because of the tension and animosity between his family and me.

I always assumed they would have preferred Tyler to have favoured my sister Amelia. With her beautiful golden locks, her social demeanour and lack of general awkwardness. So it was easier for him to stay at my place where finally my family had gotten over the fact that I was able to attract a man such as Tyler.

I began to walk around Tyler's room, gracing everything with my fingertips. I began opening his wooden wardrobe in an instant I was overwhelmed by the intoxicating scent of his clothing. I quickly undressed and threw on his grey letterman jacket, the collar still dosed in my perfume and splotches of my au naturel makeup.

I sat back in the single bed, pulling the covers over my knees. I thought about the park as I dwindled over what he had propositioned me with in his letter. The park was almost exactly half the distance between his house and mine. I reminisced about the night we decided to meet there for the first time following my date with Edmund. I lay back on the bed, and thought about that day in as much detail as I could.

As I sat waiting for him I markedly still remember my attention was drawn to a sound that didn't seem to be far away. His lethargic heavy feet were behind me. My heart started to race hearing someone reaching awfully close, my palms sweated despite the freezing temperatures.

I wasn't entirely sure it was him at first as I never expected he would actually show up. At the time he had a few more persistent admirers but low and behold Tyler came into view. It remarkably felt as though my usually one hundred mile an hour mind had discovered mute. In the late hour I was barely able to see him, under the few working street lights in the park.

Within seconds of him reaching me, I stood up from the bench a little too fast. Giving myself a blinding head rush. It felt as though I had eaten a ton of ice cream in one gluttonous feast. I came around to feel his hot breath beside my cold ear as he whispered in an unexpected seductive tone.

"Wow." I blushed as I felt his hot breath past my cool skin, chewing on the inside of my lip lightly. My arms wrapped around him enthusiastically. I closed my eyes clinging on to him tightly, savouring the moment before reluctantly letting go.

"Tyler." My cheeks flourishing to a bright crimson as I spoke again. "I'm glad you were able to meet me." I thought through each word before I spoke. I didn't want to give off any vibes of desperation but I was truly ecstatic to see him.

"I wouldn't have missed it for the world - is everything alright?" I felt his hand gently press against my lower back as he spoke. I chewed my lip once again. Tyler's touch was so addictively charming, I craved dose after dose of my favourite drug. I took a deep breath whilst I considered how to answer his question.

I wanted so badly to extend the affection, to rest my head on his shoulder to have him hold me, and comfort me. Even in my withering needy state, I knew that requesting too much of him too early could lead us down a path which is mainly centred on physical acts with secondary emotions. Would he push me away? The thought of rejection made my throat tighten, making it difficult to respond to his question once I had thought up an answer.

"I just get back from my date with Edmund." I whispered in a weak voice, I waited until he replied to my shameful confession. "Oh I see, how did it go?" I looked down as I spoke, I couldn't look him in the eye without losing track of my thoughts. Plus I couldn't very well look into his eyes and feed him the lie I was about to tell.

"It was good I guess, he's an amazing guy - really caring and old fashioned in his mannerisms are sort of sweet."

I still couldn't bring myself to look at him. I must be worse at lying then I thought. Without my next word he lightly lifted my chin. "If you're so happy Eva, why do you look so upset?" Was it really that obvious? I pondered that for a long moment, almost too long. I remember him clearing his throat to gain back my attention.

"Tyler, I just don't ever think I can be happy here, I honestly don't." I carefully analysed his reactions to my every revelation. Shivering now, he quickly noticed my trembling, feeling his arm tightened around my waist. I couldn't contain my desires but had no other choice. Allowing my craving consume me wasn't an option, but if I wanted to cling to my sanity, I at least needed to be in his presence. His face was a picture of worry as he uttered the words. "Please Eva."

I couldn't stand to live in my Upper home for a moment longer, school was over, work was hard to come by. My love life was a northing more than a never-to-be-realised fantasy, in which he was the star.

I was startled by a loud knock against my bedroom door which pulled me completely from the lovely memory. The knock was bizarre in that it differed from the tuneful knock I had come to expect from my neighbours Genevieve and Kayleigh. I sprung out of my seat and stuffed the letter into my back pocket, I straightened out my sweats as I glanced up. My room instantly transforming back into my own personal gym. I was relieved when Hedwinn entered my room.

"To what do I owe this pleasure?" I smiled softly to which he did not smile back.

He guested over to the table which had suddenly appeared beyond the exercise equipment. I slowly walked toward it with a frown, with my mind thought over why he needed this formal impromptu setting. My mind raced over my actions from the last week - had I perhaps said or done something not to his liking? As we took our seats in the new large marble chairs, I looked to him with an inquisitive expression.

"Tyler Drayga is in danger." My heart sunk down into the pit on my stomach, the sound of his name punching a hole through my chest.

Hedwinn spoke again. "As easy as it would be for me not to add to your mountain of worries, you deserve the truth. We have gathered intelligence that Julia has visited Tyler's home address several times over the last 3 weeks. We both know she wasn't stopping by to exchange pleasantries. You must understand that I cannot guarantee his protection without posing a risk to myself and the coven. I know that I have  let you down by not recognising this threat sooner.

"If we set aside a task force to ensure his safety it could compromise our mission, although the information came from a reparable source, I fear this could be an ambush. This is just a hunch, something we must pre-empt. Verdon and I will discuss our options in the morning. Tyler has his reasons to loath our kind, this much is true. But his family will not be prepared for a possible attack such as this."

I finally mustered the courage to meet his gaze, vulnerable tears falling. "Hedwinn, where has this intelligence come from? Do we know Tyler's current wellbeing?" Hedwinn nodded, the second he grabbed my hand I could hear Tyler's voice so clearly.

His smooth tone penetrated my every thought, it felt so sickeningly invasive that somehow I was able to hearing his extremely personal thoughts - how was Hedwinn doing this? Every excruciating detail was being compressed into my mind.

Tyler's intimate words were being passed through the hand of Hedwinn; how the hell was he doing this? I hadn't been given the option of prevention, but I know that even if it had been offered. I'm not entirely sure I would have turned this selfish opportunity down.

"When you're told about great love, the one, the one, person who is perfect for you in every way - that person becomes a part of you. It's an unstoppable force, that consumes you - knowing about it and actually experiencing it are two completely different things.

"For me this was it, the one I'd been waiting for. The magnitude of this force was so overwhelming. I couldn't fight against it or deny it. I don't think I'd ever want too. The night I met Eva she taught me what it was to be loved in return, an emotion which would overrule all other feelings of self-doubt. All of this in a single explosive kiss. I began to question how I'd ever managed without her. Eva's cling was so tight - she fit in my arms perfectly.

"I knew this was a new the beginning, I gently pressed my finger along the mark on her arm as she slept. This symbol wasn't just an indication of who she had become - it was a symbol of what was to come. Ever since she had gotten back, things had been different, everything was about to change. The instant the rest of the world knew who she was, we would both be subject to separation. My families grudge was still unclenched. A sacrifice I was willing to give would always be my life - in exchange for a life with her.

"I knew all too well the potential consequences of her being left to her own devices. Over time she would allow her new natural instincts to drown out her human perceptions. If put into the right circumstances, who knows the damage Eva could be capable of. Our passion is against every moral I have ever been taught by my parents. To keep her secret was the only way I could keep us together.

"I was trained to defend my family and the men and women in my town, against threats of Eva's kind. And if it came to it, even kill her kind. That thought sent a reminder of agony through my body, so crippling I didn't dare think it again.

"In a way we were somewhat lucky, I'd been told the horror stories of other dissimilar breeds of vampire; this is why the war began, this is the reason we would have no alternative to running.

"After years of trying to block the memory of my bothers death it was constantly at forefront of my mind. I now felt forced into repeatedly reliving the encounter in which we were all destroyed, by a member of the Gohinease tribe. The most feared and vicious group of vampires in history - with extraordinary tracking skills. Their leader is the fastest and wisest member of the eleven strong covens, his name is Barasa.

"My brothers and I were sitting by the railway tracks late at night. My eldest sibling Max had bought some tickets to the latest music craze a band called The Roads. He was always splashing out on us he had bought these particular tickets as a surprise.

"My youngest brother Cal was speaking to a friend on his phone, we were caught off guard. We didn't have a hope in hell of getting out of there. I remember the phone was the first thing to be tossed to the ground. After that everything else seemed to happen so fast. Within an instant Cal was convulsing on the floor his whimpers turned to screams and then to deafening silence. All of our attempts at rescue him were with no success. Barasa feed on Cal until his body had become just a shell from his cracked bones. We clawed at Barasa's back and screamed for him to stop so loud that my throat phased out. I have never cried so much in my life, that isn't the way I'm supposed to remember my bother but now it's all I can think about. Cal was my best friend, I still wake up during the night screaming for Barasa to stop.

"From that day forward my family alongside the rest of the distraught community joined forces across counties with one objective - revenge. We may not be fast or strong but we had power in numbers and machinery. Within a matter of days our story had hit the national news. Before we knew what was happening we were inundated with pledges of support, our number of well-wishers and followers continued to grow.

"It was after that point my family branded us as vampire hunters. Of course no one would believe vampires killed my brother, but something unhuman had torn him apart. That much couldn't be denied. Regardless of their kind, creed or coven the Gohinease tribe weren't the only parasites we had encountered. Each coven we encountered bared a similar mark whether it be a symbolic bite, or an entwined symbol on their bodies."

Each word was a poisonous dagger aimed straight for my defenceless heart; I was dithering between my hunger, greed and desperation for his words and the horrific feeling that I was invading on Tyler's privacy on so many levels. I couldn't count them.

With that I jerked myself back from Hedwinn's grasp, finding myself in an uncompromising and painful position. Tyler's family had every right to want revenge, to kill the man responsible. To end Barasa, but now he was one of us he was part of the circle, trying to change. If he were to perish in any way possible, I'd rather he die as a shield between Julia and myself. I couldn't allow him to die at the mercy of a simple bullet.

I couldn't shake the feeling of betrayal, not just from the fact that Tyler had hidden his families past. But also that Hedwinn had kept this ability tucked discretely up his sleeve, what else was he hiding?

Both of those feelings didn't come close to the guilt cascading through my infected blood stream, I had become a member of something he hated. The very worst part was my naivety, I never asked enough questions or even thought to look deeper into the root cause of the tensions between Tyler's family and myself.

To this day I never understood how they could even predict who I would become - things are never as sinister usually as they first appear.

"Julia knows Tyler will jump at the dual chance to see you and to avenge the loss of his brother." Hedwinn said with a stern tone as I eyed him speculatively as he spoke again. "I'm sorry Eva, for as long as I remain the leader of Avalon Barasa's actions will never be condoned. We had no idea he was involved.

"Julia is the only other member of the coven with the ability to transport thoughts, speech and conversations from one person to another. If she can reach him, she will manipulate his significance to you, we cannot let this happen. Either we find him and keep him within these safe walls or we risk Julia apprehending him. She may already have found him. Verdon is making his portal checks. We will leave as soon as he returns, this will be in the early hours. We need to be careful not to run into an ambush." I yelped.

Tyler, what have I done? Now because of me, he was in the firing line. I couldn't believe that all the running from Tyler had been in vain, I actually ran towards the very people Tyler hated the most.

I had always imagined that if I was to ever see Tyler again, it would be a magnificent celebration. It could still be breathtakingly magnificent just for a completely separate purpose, keeping in mind what is still to come. Nothing beyond this point was the same and regardless of the path I decided to tread down, I was inevitably going to betray someone. Either the people who were readily becoming the closest thing I have to a family, or the man I had already crippled to within an inch of complete emotional inhalation.

I was due to play a key part in the battle to destroy Julia, risking my health to save Tyler could compromise everything, but an attack on him felt like an attack on me. I was ready to defend us both.

Hedwinn had successfully found a way to bring me back from the brink of death once before, I was in could no doubt preform the same miracle again. If circumstances called for it.

As I scrabbled over the influx of information I had been sitting opposite the man who had undoubtedly changed my life. I watched Hedwinn's lips forming inaudible words as for a moment I wondered how fast my legs could carry me. If I could reach him in time, I could in theory prevent him playing any part in this, but where would we go? Hedwinn would find us if Tyler's family didn't first, he would never come here. We would be constantly looking over our shoulders, what is to say he would even come with me?

In doing so he would have to abandon his elders in their hour of need, and he was no coward. I didn't dare to comprehend what fate we would meet if we were caught running. I will forever plead Tyler's innocence but even Hedwinn with all his strength and ability couldn't guarantee that the other covens would listen. Bringing myself back into this grey reality I bargained with Hedwinn to save Tyler, regardless of the consequences. I asked him not to push Tyler into the firing line of our former coven members, my eyes stinging with the velocity of tears.

I was completely deflated until an astonishing revelation came to light I began remembering the healing I was able to perform on Genevieve and it dawned on me. What if Tyler was targeted?

Theoretically I could use my ability to heal his still heart if Julia injured him in anyway. Of course this would come with its consequences, and I would gladly reap the penalty.

An eye for an eye. I thought back to the letter, after Hedwinn respectfully left he room I pulled it from my back pocket.

Coincidentally he had he requested I meet him on the one date that conflicted with so indefinitely with the fight. Without Tyler none of this was worth it; he knew nothing of the dangers surrounding him.

It took me all of thirty seconds to decide that I needed to find him tonight, but the journey wouldn't be an easy one. I knew Hedwinn would certainly forbid my going out alone so close to the attack date. But what Hedwinn didn't know wasn't his to worry about.

It was only a matter of time before Hedwinn's study would be left unattended. I knew his schedule as if it were my own at 6:40pm Hedwinn and Verdon would conduct one of their many border checks, before heading to the dining area.

Once I knew the coast was clear I quietly headed to the vacant study, I couldn't waste a single second. Opening the door it was as if every move I made created a deliberately loud sound.

The door creaked irritatingly loud. As I made my way through the humongous tree branches in Hedwinn's study. Within seconds I found myself at his chest of drawers. I couldn't help but hiss as the compartments containing the detailed maps I needed were guarded by a key. I tapped my fingers against the chest of drawers as I wondered how to get to the maps, remembering to make it look as though they hadn't been broken into.

It was at that point I remembered the all too convenient gift the twins had given me for my birthday, a key that opens every door it was worth a shot. I loosened my necklace, leaning over to push the key into the lock, to my amazement the draw catch unhooked.

With a grin I rummaged through the tidy compartment until I came across the maps to the circus trees and surrounding areas. After locking the drawers again I made for a hasty exit back to my room. As I stepped past the paintings in the corridor my paranoia began playing tricks on me. The faces in the portraits created what felt like one hundred eyes staring disapprovingly at me, I grumbled. At a fast pace I headed back to the safe confines of my room.

I reacquainted myself with the borrowed goods and my contraband map. Unfolding it out over my exercise bench, studying the crossed out trees no longer available. I would have to make two stops as the conjoining portals had been destroyed. I couldn't wait, the longer I stood in this room, the longer Tyler was vulnerable. I ran to the entrance hall.

The moment I arrived in the hall I was still so in awe of the mighty Circus tree. I circled it wearily as I caught my breath. Was there a specific place I had to touch? I couldn't remember exactly, my pendant was glowing an impatient shade of green. I ran my fingertips over the bark until the colour was almost blinding. Without any conscious effort my body flung into the opening transporter.

I was still embarrassingly uncoordinated but at least this time I didn't have an audience to witness my humiliation, as I flaunted through the air. Even transporting through this passage seemed to take longer than it had ever done before, I needed to be with him **now**.

With a crash I fell back to earth, with the first intake of breath the pollution filled air had become a thick distasteful covering on my tongue. Without knowing it I had become accustom to the clean pollution free ecosystems of Avalon. Within a week of being away from my Upper home. I didn't miss my phone nor did I miss my once adored mini cooper. Not even my access to social networks to which I was previously addicted.

Thankfully my half breaded body allowed me the luxury of only having to take a breath every half hour. This blessing kept me from coughing sporadically, how had it come to this?

As I wondered though the poppy field I pulled out my borrowed map, with it I was able to see just how close I was the next portal. The next portal would take me to only a few hundred miles away from Tyler's house. I shoved the map into my backpack, straitening it out when I remembered I still needed to return it in a reasonable condition if nothing else.

I knelt down to tie my laces as I thought out my route, so long as I stayed north I would hit the portal in 4 hours, I told myself. Just stay north, I knew that once I had found the portal Tyler's scent would guide me to him. I just needed to get there with my laces now tied and my hair put back into a slick bun, I began making tracks.

Running towards the forest, nightfall was already looming overhead, it would make getting back an ordeal. With that in mind I created myself little reminders along the way, making my later return to Avalon just that much easier. I carved the barks of trees every few hundred miles with the rather appropriate letter 'T' to symbolise the right path. Apart from marking my progress on nearby trees, I did not stop.

After a few hundred miles I could no longer feel nor could I accurately see my legs beneath me, they were just a blur of repeatable movement. In my unwavering attempt to get to Tyler's as quick as I was able, I found myself beginning to test my reactions as various prey flew past me, deer's and foxes alike. I was yet to get a taste of such animals, I would have to wait longer for such opportunities today wasn't the day.

Before I knew it I had ran past 2 separate camps of families, and a local group of scouts who were earning their badges in what seemed to be a first time outing. Their chatters kept me company as I continued running, losing the sound at fifty yards out. In my absentmindedness I tripped over a rock camouflaged as an innocent moss pile. I wished so much that I could no longer feel my feet as my toes throbbed, my jeans had stained with a potent green. The left side of my face had itself become a picture of my wooded surroundings, I had been pained with the mud I had fallen into. Brilliant. Flexing my toes as I waited until the pain had mercifully subsided. If I had allowed myself more time I could have brought supplies, bandages perhaps or even just a few sashes of Crazors blood.

But at this point time was a valuable commodity and I knew the kitchen would have been occupied by the twins, and I didn't want to explain why I needed the supplies so close to meal times. I suppose I could have allowed for a few more minutes to allow the banquet to finish in order to make my escape.

Pulling myself back together I checked the map once again, not long now, just a little while. As I took a few steps forward a faint red light appeared at the nape of my neck. My pendant was confirming my suspicions, I really was already so close to the portal, leaving another reminder before shooting off I was surprisingly closer then I had originally anticipated.

In less than fifty yards I had found the familiar binding bark, I took an indulgent moment to pull out my compact. The small mirror revealed my earlier thoughts, as I tried to remove the dirt with my sleeve I heard a shuffling in the trees behind me. The sound didn't carry a scent I recognised from the creatures I had bypassed on getting to this point. In slowed motions I placed my things back into my backpack and gripped the tree trunk. A bloody red cascaded over my eyes, as I rocketed through the air at a frighteningly high speed. I strained forcing my body to stay vertical, I couldn't take another hard landing.

I had almost managed it, when again I fell sideways onto the grass almost spraining my ankle as I tried to steady myself. Once gravity had achieved its finest work in bringing me back to earth with a thud, I stood carefully to my feet. To my bewilderment the nearby odours were bombarding me, it was overwhelming, I could almost taste the nearby inhabitants on my tongue. I didn't even have to think about his location, I knew exactly where he was.

It was as if my scenes had provided me with a map with my own unique focal point, Tyler's house. To be honest I wasn't worried about anyone seeing me, I could barely see myself reflected in the array of bay windows at this speed. I didn't care for the buildings I was sidestepping or the people they contained. I was my own volcano ready to erupt if anything dared to get in my way. Only stopping once to allow my half human lungs to oxalate then darting off again as soon as I was able, the next stop I made was when I had reached his huge house. I stood outside waiting to hear the loud voices or the TV blaring from Tyler's room, but the street was deafeningly silent.

I ran as fast as I could until I was stood at his garden gate, I clung to the wooden fence outside his house catching my breath. Continuing to wait in the naive hope that he would emerge, the street lights hanging over me were the only lights to be seen.

The usually buzzing household was now a hollow empty shell, there isn't a single cell of life existing behind these walls now. I walked up the steady steps to the door, the welcome mat covered with unopened mail addressed to Tyler and his family. Amongst the junk was a postcard from Tyler's Australian friend, who he had met on holiday as a child.

I once again utilised the key attached to the chain around my neck to gain entrance to the house, I tried to flick on the switch to the kitchen to illumine the room but the electricity was cut. It didn't take long for my eyes to adjust in the darkness, as I closed the door behind me. I wondered around the empty kitchen, stripped of all its appliances and character. I took the stairs to Tyler's room, as I opened his door tears were pulling at my eyes, this was not his bedroom anymore.

It was simply a room with possessions he no longer had any need for, opening his closet I was surprised to see half of his clothes still hung on their hangers. He must have left in a hurry, I emptied all the extras from my bag to make room for his things. He may not have wanted them but they were all that remained of the man I missed so much.

As I took a more in depth look around his room, it became clear he had discarded more than just clothes. There was so much that had been considered as nonessential items, including his year books and his extensive DVD collection.

Unassumingly I rummaged through all of the dusty items played out on his TV stand and found that he had taken all of his artwork. Including the drawings he created of me. I smiled slightly with the knowledge that I was still considered a necessity to him, in one way or another. I took a few seconds to soak in the scent of him that still lingered in the room. I knew he was safe above all else and nothing else mattered.. I took a quick look through the other drawers finding nothing, Tyler wasn't one to leave things out in the open. With ease I lifted his mattress from his bed to ensure he hadn't hidden anything worth finding. My eyes widen as the newspaper clippings were revealed against the bed frame. I grabbed a handful of papers and dropped the mattress back into the frame. I glanced at one article after another 'SERIAL KILLER STILL AT LARGE' I wish I didn't know better. At least you can catch a killer, but how do you stop an army of vampires?

I doubt Julia would have given him the opportunity to pack before snatching him, Tyler was surely long gone but by sister Amelia wasn't too far away. I needed show my face and I doubt another opportunity like this would come along anytime soon. I opened Tyler's window and jumped back down from the second storey to ground level, upon looking up to gain my bearings. I was met with the astonished face of a young child, her pink pyjamas reflecting in the streetlight beside her bedroom. The girl was awake way beyond what I would consider a normal bedtime for a child of her age. The toddler was peering out of her pink daisy patterned curtains, I knew she must have seen me jump and the unusually immaculate landing which followed. I waved awkwardly to the blonde child whose chubby face was pressed against the window, creating repetitive condensation against the glass. She slowly waved back and smiled as her hair stuck slightly to the glass as she climbed down from the windowsill.

I knew eyes were on me now and with this in mind I walked at a relative *human* pace away from Tyler's house.

As I walked closed to my sister house, my mouth hung open. Tied to lampposts, fences and doors were pictures of me. The posters stated that I was missing! Not only did the poster state a reward for information but my last known whereabouts! I ran around the entire village tearing up the posters, although I was humbled. I was also terrified for those who dared look for me. I tossed the torn up leaflets into a public recycling bin.

Marching towards what was once my home I thought about Tyler and what had become of him. Why would he have asked me to meet him next week if he was planning on ditching? I thought about his large family, had they had a tip off from the wider vampire hunting community?

I hoped not. At last I found myself on the driveway of parent's house, I took a few steps back and launched myself up towards my sisters second storey bedroom window. Loudly knocking against it twice before letting go of the ledge. I glimpsed up at the moon in an effort to judge the time, I glanced back to the window as it began opening outward. I chewed my lip as a glowing Amelia appeared though the hatch.

"Eva! Oh my god! Finally! What the hell happened to you? Why haven't you called? Does mom know your back?" Oh god, the questions were starting early tonight and she wasn't even giving me the opportunity to answer. It was at that point that I became aware of the snoring coming from my parent's master room but I hadn't come here for a reunion of sorts. I hoped Amelia hadn't woken them both with her squeals.

"Shh! You're going to wake them, please just come open the door." I smiled as I patiently waited, listening to her slowly making her way down the stairs till at last she was at stood the houses entrance. My eyes widened as her bump was much bigger then I had anticipated, she pregnant alright. Her bump was humongous, she had always been the skinnier one. Her lime green dress complimented her new figure. I stepped into the doorway and hugged her delicately, as my arms wrapped around her I couldn't help but think of the last time I'd felt so close to my sister.

After I had closed the door behind me I followed behind her into the warm living room, she was still as elegant as ever. As I stepped further inside, I couldn't have imagined what a difference a few months away from here could feel like.

This house used to be my prison, one which I never thought I would be free of. The red flowery wallpapered walls, the black wooded Ikea furniture, the pointless bowls of pebbles scattered around the room. Nothing had changed, except my point of view, it felt less like a home to me than it ever had before.

Amelia took a seat on the brown leather sofa, red cushions supporting her back as she rested her hand against the bump. I glanced down to her slightly swollen feet and waited until she was comfortable to speak.

"I'm sorry I haven't been in contact, I heard I was going to be an aunt and I had to see it for myself." Amelia typically ignored my attempt to divert her from asking the inevitable obvious questions, to all of them I wasn't really sure I had the answers that she was desperate to hear.

"Where have you been? What happened with that woman? Did she hurt you? Have you been with her all this time?" I took a breath hoping she would too.

"I haven't been with her, she isn't for you to worry about Amelia. I'm so proud that you got away when you did, you have no idea what it lead to." She looked to me with her typical sceptical expression. "Try me." I sighed "You wouldn't believe me even if I told you, but I just wanted to let you know that I'm doing good and all is well."

She must have been tired as she believed my blatant lies; I wasn't even trying too hard to mask them.

"I told our mom and dad, I knew no one else would believe me. Dad quit his job to spend more time searching for you. He hasn't stopped searching and campaigning since we were taken. I knew you were alright I could feel it, I guess it's a sister thing. Tyler's family had been over here a lot, they of course believed my story, our mom and Tyler's have spoken almost every day. I guess they bonded over their missing children."

She took my shaking hand between hers, you'd think I would be fully familiar with guilt now and how it can choke you in an instant, but this was excruciating.

"Tyler has been here, when did you last see him is he alright? I can't believe dad quit his job to look for me, how is mom coping?"

I looked back up from our joined hands to gage her reaction. "I'll tell Dad you were here so don't worry, Mom is okay I guess she knows you're a strong girl. I saw Tyler about a week ago, he seemed alright, quiet as usual. He spend most of his time in your room." I groaned, completely paralysed to say or do anything.

With that my silence remaining my sister kissed my forehead and offered me a few facial wipes. I gratefully took it to clear away the mass of earth which was still masking my skin, I smiled. I declined her offer of a hot shower I knew that would surely wake everyone, my sister offered me a decaffeinated tea before I left. She began talking about gossip around the town and how dreadful I looked for someone who was supposedly. I could hear my father's snores come to an abrupt halt. Then the tick of his bedroom light switching on, I took a deep breath as I then heard my parents' bedroom door opened upstairs.

With my cowards hat firmly on my head, I dashed out the door and ran down the street before my father had reached the stairs. Most importantly had gotten away before my sisters could stop me. She would have made me stay to face my parents, I wasn't ready for that.

Once I was finally clear from my parent's village I thought about tracking Tyler down. On the other hand if the state of his house was anything to go by he was deliberately making it difficult for him to be found. I had already crossed so many lines with him and his family I wasn't prepared to cross another. With that I made my way back to the concealed Circus tree, by the time I arrived at the kingdom. I was conscious of the time and careful to ensure I could return without detection. I knew trying to place the maps back tonight would be a mistake. I kept them hidden under the mattress in my bedroom until morning.

I knew that trying to place the maps back in Hedwinn's room tonight would be a mistake. I kept them hidden under the mattress in my bedroom until morning. Laying in my cosy bed - my room was as tranquil as a hot beach on a Caribbean island.

That was the best night's sleep I have ever gotten since arriving in Avalon. Just knowing he was safe had given me much needed peace of mind. I can't even remember dreaming or the process which lead to sleep.

At the breakfast table I received a few awkward glances from the twins in particular, in less than a minute of me taking a seat Kayleigh was already whispering over to me.

"We missed you last night, where were you?" I toyed with the food on my plate as I thought of a believable excuse.

"I fell asleep early that's all." As I spoke the twins rolled their eyes at me - unlike my biological sister they were not so easily fooled.

# 9. FIGHTING FOR HIS LIFE

I was learning romance was a tricky thing to disguise between the historic walls of Avalon. After a few days it became clear that Morgan had taken a particular liking to Kayleigh. Outside of Kayleigh's designated training hours they would spend every possible moment with one another, much to the speculation of the rest of the coven.

Talking, flirting and laughing with each other until all hours had become a regular occurrence. Most irritating of all, they had begun to leave each other handwritten notes around the kingdom. Each letter contained a love poem, the pair were practically joined at the hip. It was pleasant to see Morgan had settled in so well, but we didn't really need to see everything. I have never favoured public displays of affection, although it was rather mesmerising to see the pair together, it gave us all something to celebrate.

Kayleigh had helped Morgan tremendously, he was recovering well, but he had missed far too much of the training for him to get on board. If anything he had helped us all with his own victory. Moral had been up since our visit to Balistra. We all felt completely unbeatable not to mention he had given Kayleigh more reason to fight and return home safely. Not that she really needed additional motivation - none of us did. But if you ask me, the desire we all had was not constricted to any one persons need or a particular want. It felt as though our collective desires were a strong momentum charger for one unifying request to be fulfilled.

I used my personal desire to fuel my hunger for a world without destructive beings such as Julia, but I also harboured it to give me hope. I wished for a day in which current covens would bare tolerance for my relationship with human Tyler. But I could only fight one battle at a time.

Hedwinn had decided that once we reach the Gohinease coven's kingdom, we would then depart into our designated parties. By staying together we would certainly be stronger but also a much easier target, if hit by an ambush.

The only rule enforced prior to leaving was that I accompany Hedwinn, initially I was outrageously insulted; as if I needed to have minder with me at all times. Was I that much of a hindrance?

Thankfully I later found out that Hedwinn didn't trust anyone else to protect me. After Hedwinn and Christina I was next on the prime target list. If it wasn't for Christina's amazing speed and ability to always be one step ahead in combat, she wouldn't have been allowed to accompany us. After all if Christina dies Hedwinn would die with her as stated in their marital vows - Julia knew this.

I never really fully understood the dynamics for each group until the end came. In Hedwinn's group beside me, stood Fiona and her mate Barasa, Christina, Kayleigh, Verdon and the messenger of the Gohinease coven Kaylum. He like our messenger was keen to stick with other members of his coven. Even though I sensed he was reluctant to spend an extended period of time in my particular company.

The second group consisted of a few members from the Phethlim tribe, along with the wiser members of our coven and Aluma. Alongside Genevieve, Sam and his few friends from the Gohinease tribe.

Both Twins hated the that they would have to remain separate throughout the searching process or until both targets has been confirmed dead. Their telepathic connection was the easiest and most secretive way to pass messages between the groups without any unwanted interception.

The days were becoming shorter it was as through the sand was running too quickly through the thick glass. So thick that I couldn't break it. I wanted to hold out my hands to try and stop the speed of time.

Although my body was physically ready for what was about to hit us, my emotions were yet to catch up with me. On the eve of the battle, we all drowned ourselves in Crazors blood and raised our glasses to toast of our impending victory. We filled our backpacks with sashes of Crazors blood, some canisters of water and a change of clothing. Christina was prepared for any eventuality, on her back she insisted on taking enough food and cooking equipment to feed a small army.

Hedwinn predicted that it would take a maximum of 3 days to locate one if not both of the pair. We recognised that one would never stray far from the other for very long.

The supplies we packet equated more than enough to get through the battle. But there was no guarantee that the portals would be active to take us home. Once either Julia or Hedwinn gained knowledge of the others death.

In some respect it would make sense for them to strand alongside us with the Uppers, without Avalon we would all be left paralysed. On the other hand by cutting off the Kingdom they themselves would die with no one left to fight for them. One by one the vampires of Avalon would perish. With nothing remaining but ashes to prove they ever existed. Any survivors left behind would have to integrate into the Uppers' world. An impossible task for the blood gorgers and halflings like myself. I had already learnt that lesson.

It made me wonder if the bond that existed between the father and daughter was stronger than Magnus' single desire to finally claim the kingdom of Avalon for himself. Regardless of the sacrifices necessary. Whether avenging his daughter while we were slightly weaker from the first kill, would be more dominant a desire than his fixation over Avalon's hierarchy.

We all knew that actions over the next 72 hours would answer so many of our questions, for the first time. We were about to test ourselves collectively against the 2 competitors alongside their army of crazed and badly beaten stray vampires. Each rounded up, injected and most likely trained until hitting breaking point.

We had pressed all our hopes on the second team finding Magnus whilst we simultaneously took out Julia. That way the risk of the portals being destroyed was at a minimum. With each team containing a messenger we were relying on their skills to lead us to Julia and Magnus and the forces they've assembled.

Unlike the warriors beside me, I had a secondary home; I still had roots in a world other than Avalon. But for everyone else Avalon is home. No one else existed for them outside this world waiting to take them in, if the battle ended badly.

Although the burden wasn't mine to bear alone, I certainly felt it pressing down on my aching shoulders. The twins had of course designed all of our outfits with brightly coloured bands around the sleeves. The colours gave a visual aid as to who was in which group. It was useful in training, I had spent extra time with my group synchronising our movements. The last thing I wanted was to be out of time with everyone else. The slick crafted black costumes with strategically placed protective padding were incredibly comfortable and humanely durable.

Verdon had taught me to kick way above my own height which was going to be a necessity with Julia towering over me. I just hoped her stature wasn't inherited from her father's side.

Although at the time I would never have admitted it out loud, I felt rather smug with so many techniques strapped to my belt. I wasn't allowing myself to surrender to fear or anxiety, once the time had come I was ready.

We planned to plunge a dagger into each of their barely beating hearts. Then we would we each take hold of a limb, rip them apart and destroy the pieces on our return.

Even though I much preferred Verdon's suggestion putting them in cages and watching them starve to death. Verdon shared the same view as I did, neither of them deserved a quick death which Hedwinn had planned. It incredibly seemed unjustified. But we all shared the same belief that in death, an even greater punishment for them would be waiting. Far greater than anything we could accomplish.

They had both committed many unforgiveable sins in greed, selfishness and most barbaric of all, murder. In one unforgettable day I had watched Julia slaughter many innocent men.

Before getting justice for the fallen we needed to search for survivors, members of Barasa's breed could still be alive. We wanted every able body behind us, and wounds would have begun to heal by now. Before we could start the real hunt, we would have to troll through what was left of the Gohinease kingdom.

I can only imagine Barasa's reluctance to return to his Gohinease kingdom, he had left bodies behind but the volume of damage was still unclear. It must be unusual being on the receiving end of such an attack, Barasa was not normally the victim. The aggressor was his usual role.

This was the moment we had all been waiting for, everything was finally at our fingertips. Although none of us said it out loud we all knew that this would be the last time we all walked as one through Avalon. Casualties were just too inevitable to hope for anything else, we moved as a solid swift unit stepping in time with each other. Hyper filled adrenaline pumped through our bodies.

The entire coven lead by messengers Kaylum and Verdon made its way towards the Circus tree in the entrance hall. The moment we all stepped inside I was amazed that our numbers had managed to belittle the space I was usually so dwarfed by. Once the door was closed behind us a humongous gust of wind swept around our faces down to the souls of our shoes. Within myself I was fighting the urge to throw up as my stomach twisted in knots. Luckily the twins had insisted on weaving my hair after last night's energising feast, so at least it wasn't blowing onto my face.

The pendants in attendance including mine shone a bright blistering yellow. Illuminating the fierce faces around me, each one filled with the same determination which gushed through my veins.

As legend would later have it, the elder members of our coven made the decision to close all the messaging portals within the remaining circus trees. Such as the ones which allowed me to send Tyler a reassuring letter. The decision would have made the history books if such a thing existed. Since the very first activation of the trees by our ancestors not once had the portals been closed. If we were going to continue unhindered we needed absolute radio silence. If the gateway was targeted we could at least prevent anyone from accessing our outbound catalogued communications. Both past and present. These vitally included the initial messages between the other tribes and ourselves pleading for support.

Once Verdon had completed the deactivation he placed his hand between the twisted bark of the tree and we all clasped onto one another's hands, just in time as our bodies were yanked into the vortex. I flipped and separated from almost everyone in the transportation, as my limbs flailed around my body. With little in the way of grace about my actions, I forced all my efforts into remaining upright. The wind had vanished. The moment my feet - rather than my face touched the uneven and muddy ground. Hedwinn tapped me on the shoulder to congratulate me on the fact that I didn't brake anything on landing. Not even so much as my ankle or thumb! I grinned with immense pride as he spoke.

"Not bad!" I smiled and glanced around to check that everyone around me was also accounted for. As my eyes adjusted to the dim light it was difficult to see the Gohinease kingdom through the thick smoke which had engulfed every molecule of previously pristine air. Small chunks of fallen debris fell like a blanket down on our shoulders. One by one we reunited from our landing points.

The Gohinease leader Barasa hesitantly lead us along the already decaying bridge. Leading towards the wooden door which had been reduced to smithereens, hinges in a heap on the floor. We automatically split into our two teams to effectively search the ground for survivors and hopefully some rations.

Barasa had been a coward, afraid to head back to his kingdom fearing what he had escaped. However he had told us supplies still remained along with the bodies of his coven; it was amazing Barasa and his mate Fiona had escaped with their lives.

The twins, myself and Aluma followed Barasa to the east as a deflated Fiona lead Hedwinn, Christina and Kaylum headed towards the west. I was submerged in empathy.

The building didn't reflect its proud heritage, it barely emulated a poorly constructed building site. Its walls were broken and reduced to crumbling rubble. Compared with

Avalon this kingdom resembled my idea of hell, every room barred the same scars of abandonment.

It was then that Barasa lead us down into the increasingly eerie cold underground cellar. Barasa, Sam and Hedwinn all pulled back the thick steel door. The only doorway left unbeaten in the building; I was not prepared for what we were confronted with. Several bodies laid frozen on the stone carved floor. At that moment I was thankful for the dark décor, a mortified Barasa rushed to tend to the fallen members of his breed. But it was too late for all eight fatalities to be saved. The stench of death caused us all to cover our noses, the sound of heckling throats was understandable. I was having trouble keeping the Crazors blood down.

No words can come close to describing the desolation and anguish that ripped from the throat of Barasa. I tip toed across the edge of the room. I let out a scream of my own as a hand appeared from the shadows to grab mine. Just as my lungs were about to give out Kayleigh's hand reached out and clasped over my mouth. In my fear, I had forgotten that Magnus, Julia or a member of their following could be around any corner. Ready to silence us all.

I took the ice cold hand which had grabbed mine and lead it into the slight stream of light darting through the cellar. The grey marking on his shoulder assured me he was a member of Barasa's kind, a Gohinease tribe member. Barasa brushed me aside to wrap his arms around the man, who we later would discover was the only survivor of the attacks that took place.

"I did my best but I couldn't save them, when they refused to serve under the pair, no life was spared."

He wept with remorse into Barasa's arms, we took it in turns to greet and praise the man on his attempts to save the those who had been gravely less fortunate. We all took it in turns hugging the shaken man tightly.

In our groups we then preceded to scorer the rest of the building to hunt down Magnus, a furious Barasa charged relentlessly around the kingdom. He tore through what was left of the east tower with no success. We crashed into the second group, a heart broken Christina rushed back into the arms of Hedwinn. He attempted to comfort his wife along with everyone else with reassuring words.

"They're gone. We must get the message to the Phethlim tribe, even though they have not all stood with us. They deserve a fighting chance at survival. We cannot allow the deaths of our extended family to be in vain. They will all receive a rightful and honourable Savia when this hell is all over." I didn't dare ask what a 'Savia' was. I could only assume it was a form of burial service, Hedwinn's words resonated with us all.

Simultaneously we raided through the few supplies that remained within the destroyed rooms, there wasn't much that Magnus and Julia hadn't gotten their hands on. We began dividing the rations between each other and nourishing ourselves on the Crazors blood.

After what I had witnessed it was difficult to keep the liquid from making an unpleasant return, but I needed all the energy I could get my hands on. Before I knew it I had begun praying to the ancestors in the afterlife. I begged them to build their own bridges between the people we now referred to as family. They had so valiantly stood with us despite the majority of their coven ignoring our cries for help.

Almost everyone had agreed to trial a life of Crazor dominated diets, so long as they were in our company. We had no assurances of their actions beyond the battles end. It wasn't easy for sure, but they we certainly not wavering. As far as we were concerned every individual was a converted Triquil member, for the time being. Never had such a union taken place nor would it again if things didn't end well.

As the portal between the Gohinease tribe and the Phelium tribe had been irreversibly compromised. We had no choice but to tread the extensive distance on foot. The closer we got to the Phethlim's kingdom the faster our pace became. We were running with ferocious determination towards the kingdom as time was rapidly becoming an enemy in its own right.

I had seen the kingdom feature in the stunning drawings presented in the entrance hall of our home. The huge stone walls standing out so prominently against a field of green serenity. The kingdom before me was nothing like the images had suggested, the damage was brutally extensive.

The Phethlim kingdom had become host to a wrath which it's walls could not contain, completely stripped of its amour and dignity. As we proceeded ever closer to the empire the more desperate the torturous screams became. I couldn't believe that this was my actual reality, everything had just become so incredibly and inescapably real.

As we charged forward blasts of electricity were already streaming around the battered castle. The proud flags which bared the markings of the tribe had been set on fire, blowing vast amounts of poisonous grey smoke into the nights sky.

The pendant which my grandmother had given me was no longer a sweet light hearted gift. Amongst other things it became the dagger I was eager to plunge into the heart of whomever crossed my path.

Secretly, I was hoping that I would find Julia before wasting my energies on anyone else. It was chilling how desperate I had become to see the life drain from her horrified eyes. Her death was the prize I craved and hunted for.

Using thick lumps of fallen rock, in groups we were able to smash our way through the bolted down doors which were our last remaining obstacles. The irresistible scent of fresh blood made my eyes water. We blasted our way through the doors after much resistance.

Hedwinn and I entered first as shards from the destroyed glass ceiling crackled under our feet. Together we sprinted to the aid of the already fallen victims. Bodies lay dead in the entrance quarters of the Phethlim kingdom.

All 5 victims had their hearts pulverised, their eyes dismembered from their socket. 4 of the vampires had their throats slashed. The overkill was savagely barbaric and completely unnecessary. Julia and Magnus were becoming numb to their actions, the inability to help them only multiplied our motivation.

As I paid my respects to the fallen members of the Phethlim tribe. My eyes caught sight of a grossly overweight stranger of Julia and Magnus' following. The man with greying hair appeared from around the unclear corner.

Without hesitation he lunged towards me, his grubby hands grabbed onto my hair tightly. As he swing me to my feet the skin of my face stretched and cracked, causing my face to tear and bleed. In just enough time, I was able to grab the whip I had been trained to use from the small casing attached to my back. With one precise strike, his hold on me released within an instant. I had forced him to become an uncontrollable wreck convulsing on the floor.

The Fredishdine whip struck him on his right arm and the entire right hand side of his body. As he fell, the ground shook at the tremendous impact of his weight hitting the floor. Instantaneously the ground began cracking beneath my shoes as I shielded my ears from the sound with my ice cold hands.

I watched as the Fredishdine whip electrocuted every cell in his huge grotesque body. As I witnessed his eyes rolling back into his head, I effortlessly used the end of the whip to tie his hands together. I then forced the iron handle into the cracks in marble floor, securing him in place, in case he decided to try his luck and come after me once again. But after the shock he endured I highly doubted he would be walking anytime soon.

The second I wiped my bleeding brow another man ran towards me so fast that I couldn't make out the features of his face. As I poised to defend myself Sam appeared out of nowhere and tackled him effortlessly to the ground. Before I could jump in and help, a pained screech from the east had me running from the mammoth entrance hall.

The scream lead me to another smaller but equally destroyed room where at last our efforts would be rewarded.

Julia's bright grinning face came glaringly into sight, her teeth bearing down on the badly beaten carcass of a middle aged patron of the Phethlim tribe. We had arrived too late despite all the running, all the tracking and all our best efforts.

Julia's clothing was dripping with blood stains both new and old. I caught my reflection in a pile of various shards of glass beneath me. My eyes black as the nights sky, before I had even looked up she had me pinned to the floor. Her ice cold strong hands wrapped forcefully around my throat. Her grip was so chokingly tight that I could feel my gullet closing. My lungs straining for oxygen. I smelt the stench of her copper rancid breath rippling against my terrified face. Her hands clenched even tighter around my throat. I have never experienced fear so virtually paralysing.

Behind the sound of her growls, the ricochet of snarls in the distance roared through the room. The voice was so distinguished, Hedwinn was also in trouble. Bodies slamming together, the whales of another unfamiliar man followed, Magnus.

*Please Hedwinn, please be alright. Don't stop fighting.*

A red mist began descending over my eyes, stunting my internal prays for him. Julia's grip was unwavering strong despite the screams of her father close by.

My body was completely paralysed with the combination of shock and my increasing lack of inhalation. Despite everything Tyler was all I could think about, this isn't how I wanted my story to end. I wasn't about to let Julia have the last laugh, as I pictured his face in place of hers finally I found the strength to fight back.

I swung my knees from under me to shove my foot against her stomach, with all my might I kicked her body over to the opposite side of the room. Her body left a huge growing crack in the wall with the intense impact I had flung her. It was at that moment that I remembered the exact reason I had been giving the ever changing pendant. It certainly wasn't just to cross between portals. Had my grandmother gotten the opportunity to speak with Harpitunia?

I'd like to think she knew one day that I was going to do great things, this action was going to be one of many. Holding on to that powerful thought I ripped the pended from its glimmering chain. With my fist still shaking I wrapped my fingers around the shape, as Julia gained consciousness and began struggling to her feet. I stood up and marched towards her, I grabbed hair and slammed her body down onto the ground. The back of her head smashing against the marble. With force I began pressing my knee against her throat keeping her locked down.

I pressed the entire weight of my body down her as I raised my hands above my head. With as much force as I could conger up I rammed the diamond pendant into Julia's heart, repeatedly. I continued stabbing the artery violently. Warm orange blood spurted over my body and her face. Via my fingers I felt the last few beats of her heart through the pendant.

The catastrophic scream she let out shattered the remaining overhead chandeliers, Julia clawed hard at my knee for freedom with the strength she had left. Her nails dug so deep, she began tearing through the ligaments in my leg.

I yanked my pendant from her chest as a black tear fell from her closing eyes. I couldn't bring myself to look away as I waited expectantly. I was convinced the moment I looked away she would dive forward and try to take me down with her.

My limp body curved around reluctantly as I heard a bruised Hedwinn hobble his way towards me, offering his grey cloth covered hand to me. With a fair amount of ease he pulled me upwards from the soaking floor, I hugged him, so grateful that we could finally rest.

After a moment of reprieve a barely alive Magnus dragged Hedwinn away from me. Magnus looked down to his daughters dead body, instantly he roared with fury. Magnus slammed my unprotected frame against the wall.

Then almost immediately he retreated as if his attention was being pulled into another direction.

Before I could make my retort he vanished back towards the entrance hall. Bewildered Hedwinn and I quickly ran after Magnus. Despite my horrifically injured leg I forced myself to run with all my might in his direction, until I was stood outside the building's walls.

No longer haunted by Julia I took a moment to breathe but twelve short seconds later, I couldn't breathe. My entire body began internally failing, the scent I was picking up was not one of any vampire. Magnus stepped forth in the distance.

Tyler's petrified eyes never wavered from mine the moment I looked in his direction we made unwavering eye contact. Magnus was holding a blade to his mortal throat, I chocked as Tyler's delicious blood trickled down his vulnerable neck. The tip of the blade repeatedly nicked his skin.

Tyler's heartbeat was the echo to the alarm bells ringing relentlessly through my mind. I still couldn't breathe, I could do nothing but look on in desperation. I took a few steps backward as Magnus continued to drag a terrified Tyler towards me.

"I'll heal Julia, please I'll do anything, leave him alone. I'm the one you're after, **PLEASE**!" My voice was a high pitched mess as I pleaded desperately with every ounce of humility I had left.

A sadistically grinning Magnus stared at me as he slit Tyler's throat without remorse.

Everything stopped.

"**TYLER**!" I whaled the second his body fell the floor, I could no longer hear his strong heartbeat or the bird singing in the trees or the screaming of Genevieve and Kayleigh behind me. Everything suddenly became mute.

It was as if Tyler's death had drained out all other forms of life around me.

The moment I looked up from Tyler's body Magnus was already fleeing. Kaylum, Verdon and Sam ran after him.

I forced my defiant muscles into action and ran over to my boyfriend, the moment I was close to him my legs buckled beneath me. I crawled with exhaustion and devastation.

Before I could touch his dying body an unusually rough handed Hedwinn grabbed a hold of my shoulder as he feared my next move. I could barely see him through my drowning grief stricken eyes, using what little energy I had left I forced Hedwinn backwards. As he fell, I caught sight of Aluma looking down to me from a tear in the side of the Phethlim building. She simply shook her head but I knew that if anyone one else was in my shoes, for instance if Christina had been in danger Hedwinn himself would have done the same thing.

I grabbed Tyler's arm as I did so a thin silver band fell from between his fingers, frantically I pushed the ring onto the forth finger of my left hand. Without hesitation I looped my fingers back with his and began taking every ounce of pain from him. As I transferred his wounds to my body I was surrendering myself to his fate. Taking his pain was an agonisingly slow process, no matter how hard

Hedwinn tried to free our hands, I clung desperately to Tyler.

Until I began to feel my orange blood pouring down from the slit now presenting on my throat. The pain was so excruciating I closed my eyes tightly and begged for it to stop. In less than a minute I could no longer feel Tyler's hand linked with mine. I fell back onto the soft green grass, I began choking on my copper blood and my body began convulsing.

I watched a terrified awakening Tyler, he had started compressions on my fractured chest. The last thing I heard was Hedwinn's demanding overly jaded voice until mercifully my eyes closed. Nothing is ever as you expect it or indeed as you plan it.

I will always be waiting for him to find me; death should never be justified, unless of course you seize to exist for someone you undoubtedly love for this I am grateful and honoured.

But Tyler wouldn't allow me to take the fall, he was about to head up his own journey.

# 10. TYLER DRAYGA

I shouted into the emptiness surrounding me, this time last week we would have been celebrating. Not only was it her birthday but the balloon that was Amanda had finally popped.

I always knew Eva was the type of person who would throw herself beneath a moving vehicle to save a complete stranger, but this was beyond any instinctive behaviour. Despite everything, I had loved this woman for so long I didn't know how to be good at anything else. Until I receive a remotely plausible explanation, I would not give up. I often asked myself why did I have to be the man to fall for the woman who would one day be only half mortal? Why couldn't I break this bond? Snap what was left it into a million pieces.

Unlike my girlfriend, I was not host to parasites pumping through my blood nor was I surrounding myself with them. Those vampires were responsible for Max's death. The succubus' had created a war inside of me and I was fighting for both sides. Half of me wanted to save her and half wanting to loan out a lethal weapon.

My family had become a wealth of knowledge since my bothers death, if they knew I had come to find one of the largest breeds of vampire alone. My life wouldn't be worth living. It was either this or sit at home wondering what the hell went wrong, I'm sick and tired of feeling powerless.

Eva, so innocent and fragile tossed into this world of torment and rage, I hated it. Every single one of them is branded with hideous scares. Each one marking most likely representing a life they've taken. I had so much hatred ready to explode from my fists.

I was saving my energies for when I finally get my hands on Julia.

The woman in red. She was responsible for the complete destruction of Eva's life. As human beings I knew the kinds of diseases we can carry in our blood. If all was lost, I would inject that bitch with a toxin such as HIV. Killed by what she craves the most, disgustingly poetic. Although I'm not sure if the pesticides in her body would fight off the disease but either way, I would certainly have fun experimenting with different diseases.

As I called out Eva's name again I was stopped mid-sentence.

My feet dragged along the floor as a filthy hand clinched my mouth. My jaw locked between its fingers, twisting and shoving I was unable to break free. My shoes hitting against the weed ridden ground, my shrieks silenced beneath his hand. I felt the sharp prick against my neck, my breathing short and harsh as I tried to figure out that the hell was going on. - Sabotage?

Through the waves of dense smoke I could see nothing but her pale face as she starred back at me, with terrified penetrating beautiful eyes. Through the hand of the man restraining me, the sickening smell of smoke and blood singed the tiny hairs inside my nose. Eva's voice tore through the sound barrier. Eva pleaded with the man, watching her cry was worse than anything this murderer could do to me.

As soon as my body collapsed and silence followed, somehow within seconds I was breathing again; I died and was reborn within an excruciating instant.

As soon as I sat up, she was convulsing, barely conscious, I shook her shoulders, squeezing her hand. I did the only think I could do, I started preforming CPR..

My eyes straining to hold back the evidence of pain which had begun slashing up my insides. I kissed the back of her hand which now bared my mother's prize possession. I bargained with salvation to bring her back, please, please, please. I was torn between my desire to find the host responsible before he escaped and my need to help Eva.

Both circumstances were beyond my control, pressing my ear to her chest I waited for the beats. I looked up only to be met by another unfamiliar face, within a blink he tossed me aside. I growled as he pushed me away from her body, I shoved him back as my jaw tightened and my protective instincts for Eva shot into overdrive. The immortal psychopath ordered two identical women to lift her body as he held me back. I had travelled thousands of miles only to be invited to the funeral of my girl.

I tackled the tall irritating man, punching his stone face my knuckles cracking and severing with each blow to his face. My deep red blood spraying over his face with each repetitive hit. Almost mercifully he threw me aside, the idiot dislocating my shoulder as he crushed me to the ground. His disgusting black eyes glaring down on me.

"Breaking your bones will not be a valid contribute to saving her life, pull yourself together!" Once he had stood up, he grabbed my wrist and starting pulling me to my feet. My fingers were still dripping with the combination his filthy orange blood and mine. The moment I was able to speak, I did with deflation and devastation.

"Nothing can save her now, you hurled us both into an ambush. I knew your kind would do this! Nothing but cold hearted empty vessels, you'll pay for this soon enough."

My voice carrying with it more anguish then I could hold back. In seconds a crowed of them had gathered around me, the only difference this time was that I couldn't clench my fists. As the two women had taken her from me, I shouted with every ounce of hate and disgusted I felt towards each and every one of them.

"Why aren't you doing anything? You're all stood here like butter couldn't melt! He is out there, you could catch up, you filthy creators have faster legs than mine. As much as I hate to admit it, you'll find him much quicker than I ever could, GO! Don't you dare let him get away, don't you dare let her die in vain. She gave up her life up for you people!"

The same man stepped forward again. "Would you rather we invest our time chasing him, or saving Eva?" I hid my face in my hands, rubbing my exhausted skin with my shattered to pieces palms; he tapped me on the shoulder.

"Come, we have things to do." With little choice I followed the stranger into the woods. I tried my best to keep ahead, I needed to catch up those two girls carrying Eva. I was quickly getting frustrated as Eva was nowhere in sight, I took a breath as I finally caught up reaching her at last. My numb broken fingers once again finding hers.

The twins placed her down allowing the others to catch up. I sat beside her as the entire clan knelt around us, feeding themselves. The women had stripped a nearby oak tree of its bark, carefully I helped place Eva onto the amply constructed stretcher.

"You can call me Hedwinn." The man finally introducing himself. Looking down to Eva, I felt so instinctively protective. I wanted to shield her from everything. Including the people around me, the creates which inhabited these woods. And in some ways I wanted to guard her from myself. I wish I knew what she needed, who she needed. The ring she had chosen to wear was evidence enough to me that she wanted me around in some capacity. I wasn't going to make the mistake of leaving her side again.

"There is only one way we can bring her back." My heart picked up its pace, I felt it twisting and swelling at the possibility he was proposing was this a trick? Half a second ago I thought I'd be planning a burial service.

"Bring her back?" Another man, aesthetically similar to 'Hedwinn' stepped forth. "I know of a way, but if we do it we have no way of knowing what she will come back as."

I frowned, my eyes constantly glancing between the palest faces and Eva. "As her next of kin, the decision is yours." I could feel the eyes and volume of bodies around me, the choice I was given was ridiculously easy.

"Do whatever it takes." It was incredulous to me, the idea of doing nothing, they had put her here they had forced her into this existence, *they* had better fix her and fast. The man to Hedwinn's left nodded with weary eyes, looking to the rest of the group.

"You know what this means." I was not used to being the outsider, but in their company, I was the odd one out. I frowned. "What must be done?" I asked as an exasperated Hedwinn walked towards me, the others began talking amongst themselves in small huddles, each one of them was too damn quiet for my ears to take note.

"We are not all killers and murders, just like you, we live on animal meat; the only difference between us is that we're never full. Eva had chosen to join us, she has choice to stay or leave, we did not force her cohabitants. I can only apologise for Julia's and Barasa's actions but as you may or may not know she has paid the price and Barasa will be dealt with later. Now, everything from this point forth is going to be difficult.

"We cannot carry her body within the allotted time and as you refuse to leave her side, we have no option but to leave her here. Kayleigh and Genevieve's connection will be imperative."

I was getting the feeling he wasn't so much talking to me as much as himself at this point. I cleared my throat and he looked up as he began to speak again.

"We will leave her here, with you, we have food for you and Genevieve will stay also. She is strong, she can protect you both."

I glowered. "Protect us from what?" He sighed. "Not everyone is a member of my coven The Triquils. Some like those who killed your brother may come looking for proof of her death." I scowled, the idea of someone coming to obtain her body, taking her again. I couldn't bare it. I nodded as he once again drifted off into a verbal tangent.

"Whilst you 3 remain here, we will hunt down Magnus, we will require what remains of him to bring her back. I know he will not come without a fight but we mustn't dwell. If we do not reach Katrina within the next 70 hours, we have absolutely no chance of getting her back." I was stunned into silence, for a moment.

"Katrina?" His patience was a commendable quality. "She isn't from our world, though she once one of us. She now lives above the surface to be closer to civilisation and certain forms of humanity. We will have to summon her, Katrina will not be happy we're on the Upper surface. When I arrive in person she will accommodate without qualms, she will perform the ritual. However as Verdon predicted we cannot make any reliable estimations as to what characteristics Eva will come back with."

I stared down to her beautiful face I had nothing to say. My soul responsibility was to keep her safe, along with the help of Genevieve, I sighed. But before I could speak he continued.

"We have sent for our newest and strongest member, he will be returning with us." I nodded, knowing we needed all the help we could get.

"You better get going, do not come back unless you have found him." With that statement, Hedwinn and the others left me with a few packs of food and water. Hedwinn went on to introduce me to Genevieve; one of the twins. I'm interested in making pointless small talk. I'm not interested in talking to them at all, this isn't a social occasion.

This feeling wasn't mutual, the blond sat beside me once everyone else had set off.

"I never thought she was the marrying type." I sighed, I didn't want to think of her existence in the past tense, and I selected my words carefully.

"She isn't." I took off my jacket, placing it over her body sheltering her body from surrounding eyes. I browsed around in order to find some useful tools. We needed to create a shelter for her in case the weather changed. Maybe the blonde's presence will prove useful after all.

"We need to create a viable shelter, if you move the trees just arch the trees the branches and leaves will protect her from any down pours. Whilst you do that I will collect some fire wood, then I suppose I ought to eat."

She nodded, as soon as I finished speaking she began tearing and arching trees to form the base of our make shift shelter around Eva. I stayed close to her as I collected viable wood; thankfully I knew one of the few things I had packed into my pockets was a pack of matches. As I picked up the logs, I kept looking over my shoulder the distance. I was putting between her and I was becoming a physical pain.

I glanced at Genevieve as she swung high up in the tree branches, two sets of eyes were better than one let's hope she doesn't fall.

I was back beside her; luckily we had just built the shelter just in time as rain pelted down from the grey clouds. It was just my luck that the rain hadn't deterred the animals from trying to get close to the site. The smell of burning wood and warm blooded bodies was bringing out hungry foxes, racoons and coyotes, those I could fight off. I was keeping my eyes open for anything bigger. I'd have little luck with bears.

The thunder made it difficult to hear anyone approaching. I kept huffing hot air from my mouth between my hands, rubbing them together trying to keep myself warm. Genevieve had gone unusually quiet, at least I thought she had.

Her vacant expression kept me wondering.

"They're so close to catching him." I raised my brow. "Already?" She nodded. "Hedwinn and Verdon are very good at tracking others, we look out for our family, Tyler. Which by extension means that whilst I am in your company, I am responsible for your welfare. Here drink this."

The woman handed me a hot steaming mug, I sniffed it curiously. Tea. I nodded. "Thank you" I carefully plucked a few bugs and insects from my jacket which covered Eva. After nightfall, Genevieve and I took shifts, thankfully she could function on 15 minutes of sleep, but those minuets felt like hours. I starred at Eva's lips willing them to intake air but no such miracle occurred.

For a second I allowed myself to think about her soul. I knew she had firm beliefs regarding life after death. I smiled at the thought of her reuniting with her grandmother. A woman I know Eva has missed dearly since her passing, she talked about her all the time. Selfishly I hoped she was missing her life here, and me.

"God Eva, I miss you." I mumbled until finally I was able to sleep.

The blond woke me up by shaking my shoulders with her bony hands. The sun hadn't even rose yet and she was already wailing. I looked over my shoulder to see Eva, undisturbed.

"What the hell are you playing at!?" I growled. "They have reached Magnus, they have injected him with the anaesthetic, and at least the easy part is over!" I frowned. "The easy part?" She nodded as I sat up, my body aching from laying on the floor all night.

"Yes, we knew finding him would be easy after all he was wounded from Hedwinn's earlier attack. He was practically a moving target. Now we have to reach Katrina before sundown, the ritual takes time. If Eva returns, we have no guarantee's she won't come back with more of his characteristics than we could ever bargain for."

Genevieve just looked at me almost cynical of my initial decision to opt for such extraordinary measures, it's a shame the shoe isn't on the other foot; at least one part of the mission was complete. Part of me knew Eva wouldn't want any of these extraordinary measures, if anything she would hate that we were resting here like sitting ducks, whilst the others tried to make good on their promise.

I also knew she would have insisted on exemplary measures, if I had been lying in her place right now like I should have been. Eva had barely lived, she had existed for all of nineteen years she deserved more, was entitled to so much more. And if I'm honest this damned world wouldn't be worth jack without her in it.

The blond kept offering me beverage after beverage, as if it could stop my relentless pacing. I couldn't stop myself from going through each stage of the hazy plan in my head. I watched Genevieve brush some hair from Eva's face, removing dead leaves which had fallen from our makeshift shelter. I signed knowing that Eva would hate the attention. She never was a cosmetically enhanced woman, she didn't need it. I loved her jean wearing, t-shirt loving tousled style.

"Love." I corrected myself out loud, looking over to Genevieve who was eyeing me suspiciously over my seemingly random statement. She was keeping warm beside the fire, although the sun was up the temperature wasn't.

When Genevieve wasn't combing her hair or telling me about the place that Eva had inhabited over the last few months. She was communicating with her twin sister, telepathically. The more she told me about Avalon the more I began to understand Eva's devotion to the 'kingdom.'

I couldn't match that place nor could I stand against the people within it.

"Only a few hundred miles until they reach us." She grinned. "You've been saying that for the last hour." I replied. I couldn't see Genevieve as my back was to her as I tended to Eva, but I already knew she was rolling her eyes at my response. I could hear the packet containing blood ripping open in her greedy manicured hands, I groaned.

Another day in paradise surrounded my blood hungry parasites; I didn't much feel like eating.

The sound of my cracking knuckles and my impatient footsteps around Eva was the only sound in an otherwise unusually quiet forest. Much to Genevieve's annoyance.

Until flamboyantly she jumped across the camp side to greet the other members of team who had at last emerged. Carting with them a gurgling man dressed in bloody rags. It wasn't until he was thrown to the floor that I was able to recognise him.

Hedwinn walked over to me, creating a physical barrier between my ready to explode fists and my girl's killer.

"You should eat, you look like hell." I clenched my teeth. "I'll eat when she does, so what next?" I asked.

"We eat, rest for half an hour, give him another dosage just before leaving." He tilted his head to the now silent Magnus.

"Then we make tracks towards Katrina, the portal isn't too far from here, as you know. If it's alright with you I would like to speak with you beforehand. That is if Genevieve hasn't worn your ears out already? Come."

175

S L Dixon

More talking? I held back an impatient hiss. At least I would only have to endure it for half an hour before heading off. I sat wearily beside him. Hedwinn began probing the fire with a large tree branch, jolting it back to life. "It's no coincidence you showed today is it?" I shook my head.

"How did you know our location and more importantly how did you get through the portals?" Hedwinn kept his shoulders back at all times, it was like talking to a sergeant.

"With this." I held up the pendant which had arrived at my house, Hedwinn examined it for a moment before taking it from me, frowning.

"You stole this, from under her nose?" I chuckled. "No of course not, it was delivered to my previous address along with a letter." I glanced over to Eva for a second to check she was safe, before reaching into my back pocket. Taking out the letter which was hand written and personally delivered by Julia whilst I was out of the house. Hedwinn pulled apart the letter, pressing out the creases on his knee, reading it out loud.

"Tyler, I have something belonging to you, but not for very long, take this and head west until you see the pendant turn blue. Find the circus tree and think off the one you love. If you ever want to see her again that is. See you soon."

Hedwinn looked at me with a smile. "Do you mind if I keep these?" I shrugged. "They're of no use to me now." He nodded as I handed him the pendant.

"Very well, we better get going."

"I'll carry Eva." I interjected. "By yourself? That's noble, but completely unnecessary Verdon and I can manage, don't worry. The twins did a tremendous job with the stretcher. If we grow tired, as promised I brought along our stronger and youngest member to support us through the rest of this journey, she's in safe hands. Your job is done for the day, you can relax now. Here eat this."

He tossed me an apple. It wasn't the stretchers stability that I was worried about, Hedwinn stood folding the letter in half and then again. I watched him hand the pendant over to a perplexed Verdon as I got to my feet. I watched as they lifted Eva's body, feeling helpless again. I grabbed Eva's belongings along with the my own. I tossed some of my water over the fire and waited whilst everyone else regrouped.

Once we had set off, the relationships within the group became more obvious. Myself stood beside Eva, Christina and stood beside Hedwinn, the twins never separating. Verdon beside Kaylum, Fiona beside Barasa and two another males followed us all, so eager to please. I wasn't sure which one Hedwinn called 'the youngest and strongest' but I took a guess. After he was done his round talking to everyone else, he made his way towards me, but I wasn't in the mood. Not unlike every one of them, he is so enthusiastic and relentlessly merry, even at a time like this, I can't understand it. It was exhausting to watch.

"You've got yourself a good one there; I would have made the same decision, save your strength." The man offered me his hand, begrudgingly I shook it.

"Any friend of Eva's is a friend of mine." I frowned. "Friend?" He hit his head with the palm of his hand, rolling his eyes.

"Damn! You two are engaged right? That's cool, so how does it feel to be the new guy? Sucks doesn't it? But everyone is sweet, especially your gal. She helped me out a lot in the beginning and boy did I needed it."

My Gal? I squeezed the handles on my backpack with my hands to stop my tired fists from punching his too perfect pale face; I didn't dignify his idiocy with a response until I had calmed down. "New guy? I don't think so, as soon as all of this is put right, and she is back to her senses we are getting out of here.."

The idiot almost tripped over his own feet "We?"

I hastily walked on, as fast as my legs could carry me thankfully he didn't follow me. But after a few hours my legs felt like I was lifting led. I was just about keeping sight of the vampires ahead of me. I kept fighting against all my instincts which were telling me to stop before I fall.

But I couldn't stop. Losing sight of them meant losing sight of Eva and I wasn't letting that happen, not again.

That bugger Morgan is persistent; after I slowed down to an almost crawling pace, he never strayed from my side.

"Let me take those bottles, I have room in my backpack. I can tell you're exhausted, at this rate you won't make it another mile." After his repetitive persuasion, I finally gave in and handed him a few litres of water. I didn't however give him Eva's things or my drawings I'd kept. Those were my responsibility with the reduced weight along with my intake of food and water, I was able to keep going. My clothes covered in sweat as we finally pitches up the hills.

"How did you know? I mean other than the physical differences, how did you know Eva was changed?"

I smiled at the memory Morgan's question had triggered.

"She kept sneaking out at night, I was terrified she was cheating, but I knew there had to be another explanation. As it turned out she was heading to the local library every night, reading up in myths and legends. She was checking out some unusual literature. After that we had very few heated discussions about it" He frowned "Sorry I asked."

"Don't be, I love talking about Eva, I'm Tyler by the way. What about you? How did you end up here? You said something about being a new guy?" He smirked.

"End up here? You make it sound like a terrible thing. I fought for my place here. It nearly killed me but I would do it all over again without a doubt. Man, you should have seen it. The best day of my life and that's saying something!" My face automatically twisting as I nodded.

"Defiantly something awful in the blood of the animals around here." I muttered sarcastically beneath my shallow breath, to which he did not reply. Instead he gave me a sour look, I think I killed his buzz.

"Almost there now." He lifted his necklace, identical to the one every other one of them was wearing. Except now it was glowing like it had done when I found my way here. I put two and two together, finally we were headed up top, back to where people were just people. Lights are just lights and blood was not to be consumed; back to where things made sense. Ignorant bliss.

I helped as we took Eva from the stretcher; Hedwinn took her into his arms shielding her with his coat. Barasa threw a still unconscious Magnus over his shoulder, Fiona squeezing his hand.

"Aluma will meet us at the other end with a separate stretcher she has built, everyone take hold."

I grabbed on with everyone else, like before I slammed my face onto the floor as we landed. Except this time I was not met with warm grass but unbreakable concrete. They all stood beside me pulling my face from the ground. The left side of my face and ear had taken the main force of my landing. Their mouths didn't coincide with the muffles I was hearing, Morgan pulled me up.

One of the women I had barely spoken with began patting my face with a clean white cloth.

I couldn't help wincing again and again.

"Son of a bitch!" I hissed as the water she pressed against my skin only added to my pain. Finally everyone backed off, giving me a chance to gain some bearings. This is after all my territory.

"I'm Christina, hold still. You've got yourself a nice bruise there, that's going to sting, here drink this." The same women handed me the clear plastic bottle, I glanced inside to check it was clear liquid. I took a swig before placing the lid back on top, the sun was set high in the sky obstructed by the clouds confirming that we didn't have long. I watched as they rested Eva onto the stretcher, an elder woman walked towards me, checking my wound.

"Give it a few days, you'll be good as new, you Uppers are frightfully fragile." She shuddered and walked off to speak with the men. The elderly woman was not like elder woman in my world. At her age you'd think she would be wrapped up in blankets drinking tea and watching soap operas. Not bossing around younger men and now spearheading the operation to bring Eva back. Everything was different underground.

I didn't dare touch the bruise as it continued to pulsate, I could see from the corner of my eye my face had swollen into an unattractive lump. Now they weren't the only ones baring a disgusting mark on their body now I did too. Finally I felt like I belonged, or not.

Before I knew it we were walking again, I was rather grateful for my slight loss of hearing as the conversations started up again.

This time the elder woman was the focus of everyone's attention. She was leading the way, from what little detail I had gathered she was the one who knew the most about the woman we were desperate to find, Katrina.

It felt so unusual, walking so close to the streets I had grown up in, yet I felt like such a tourist. The people within the nearby houses are so oblivious to the things I knew and to the people I was walking with. I felt so envious of absolute normality.

"The harbour isn't too far." I groaned at the prospect of sitting on a swaying boat with my head already spinning. But this was just another part of the journey to bring her back, I got on-board with everyone else willingly.

"The southernmost boarder, it shouldn't take long, I have had the engine refuelled and ready to go." Aluma stated.

I forced my legs to move faster, the sun was a beady ever moving eye looking down on me. Forcing time to push by faster.

I climbed onto the boat, following Eva's body and the rest of the team. As soon as I sat down, I began to feel the excruciating ache of my muscles and the stinging of my cheek.

I took a seat bedside Eva, taking her hand into mine I didn't mind the Goosebumps from her cold withering skin. I kept my head down as the engine was fired up with so many people on board. I couldn't get a moments peace, to comprehend what was going on and what was coming next. As the small boat skipped its way over the sea, I felt my empty stomach twisting into knots and releasing as we hit another wave.

"**Look out!!**" Screamed Fiona, clinging on to the arm of a stern unaffected Barasa.

The boat named 'Aluma' swerved violently towards the left; I gripped onto the stretcher keeping it from going over board until we were back completely horizontal.

I looked at both Barasa and Fiona, unlike everyone else they did not hold the same items, nor did they have the same marks, pure vampires. Hedwinn had told me justice would be served for those two, once we had recovered Eva. Never in a million years would I have thought I'd be sitting opposite the man who killed my brother. Although he acted and looked like a different 'person' I knew the truth he was so desperately trying to hide. No matter how much I wanted to kill the bloodsucker, I will wait until he has served his purpose in bringing Eva.

Barasa and his mate looked just as hungry as I am, it made me sick. I swallowed hard, taking a drink of water from the bottle Christina had given me. I swear I can feel the liquid swishing around in my bottomless pit of a stomach.

After forty unsettling minuets, the boat began to slow down, the eldest woman along with everyone else crowded around stood at the nose of the boat. Each of them pointing the way, shouting orders back to an obedient

Verdon. It wasn't until the engine stopped that was able to stand up, we had at last made it.

"Not long now baby." I whispered to Eva as I kissed the back of her hand.

The frightful scene around me wasn't as I had expected. We reached an ugly worn out harbour. All I could see was one small cottage inhospitably situated in the middle of nowhere. Black smoke bellowing out from a small chimney, beside the cottage was a small water mill, churning away in the background. On the slanted roof sat a dozen ravens, some with mice squealing between their beaks and others looking down on us as though we were their next meal.

Hard lashings of wind kept hitting my face but even that didn't contrast in temperature to the pale hand I was still holding. As we stepped out one by one, the small wooden harbour swelled and creaked beneath our feet against the weight of our bodies. The polished streamlined boat looked freakishly out of place against the tired backdrop. I scrutinised Hedwinn as he began lifting Eva's body from the stretcher.

Walking over to him I stated. "I can take her from here." He nodded and carefully we made the exchange, once she was securely tucked up in my arms we all followed the elder woman up seventeen steep stone steps towards the cottage. All we needed now was a dash of lightening and I would truly feel like part of a low budget horror film set in the 1960's.

Eva felt so light in my arms, too light, her head still cradled into my shoulder. "We only have 67 minutes, she's expecting us." The elder woman speaking whist making a few sobering knocks on the black door. After several seconds it creaked open to reveal a large elderly man, his breathing heavy as he took a bite into stale mouldy bread. Crumbs dropping into his grey beard as he chewed. His thick bifocals exposed every movement of his eyes as he scanned our faces, his mouth still full.

A thin hand gripped his shoulder and with that he stepped back, an equally elderly olive skinned woman invited us in. Only 5 of us had entered when she waved her hand again.

"Only 4, including the two." She looked at Eva, then at me, pausing as she looked into my eyes. "The rest of you will have to wait elsewhere." I wasn't going anywhere, Morgan handed Hedwinn Magnus' battered body. One by one everyone else made their way back towards the wreck of a dock.

I had a feeling this place was ready to be torn down, the revolting smell of freshly court fish and sea salt seeped in from the harbour into every open nook and cranny. Absolutely everything was covered in rodent droppings, the floor was scattered with unsuccessful mouse traps, covered in mouldy cheese. Through the single pane battered windows, I was able to taste sea salt on my tongue; I tried to hold my breath. Each agonising second was echoed through the room as buckets dotted around the house had another droplet of water to hold from the leaking roof, I shivered.

"We don't have long Katrina." Stated Aluma before turning to close the door behind her as we were led down more steps. We were now beneath the crumbling floor boards. I held onto Eva's hand tightly until I was asked to let go. I had to place her body beside his on two tall platforms.

Ever since we had placed the bandages over Eva's throat; I had done everything and anything I could not to think about the pain I knew she felt. It was never hers to take.

"How does this work?" Hedwinn and I were both thinking the same thing; I just came out and said it.

"Is she going to wake up in pain?" Katrina waited for a long moment before she responded.

"Let's just hope she wakes up at all, Mr Drayga."

I didn't know she knew my name, but nothing came as a surprise to me now. The woman's accent was strange, it was certainly not from around this corner of the county. She sounded Scottish. Understanding her was practically impossible. As she walked towards their bodies her long white stained night gown draped over the animal droppings on the floor. As she spoke again her yellow stained teeth were exposed, nothing about this felt safe. Eva's life is in *this* woman's hands. Is there no alternative?

"Whilst his heart is still beating we need to take several pints of blood and extract the adrenaline, as the transfusion is made I will stop his heart and take a piece, where is the others pendant?" Hedwinn held up both the pendant I had given him handing it over to her.

"Poor destructive soul." Katrina said quietly as she studied Julia's pendant. "So young." She shrugged and placed the necklace onto a hook beside Magnus' head, the woman stuck a needle into Magnus arm. The drugs or whatever Hedwinn had given him had certainly knocked him out. He didn't acknowledge the needle was stabbed deeper, I leant against the wall as I was no longer able to support my own weight without swaying.

I felt sick. As his blood drained, she inspected Eva's pendant, continuously glancing to me she kept it locked in her hand. She began scrutinizing Magnus' deep red blood, it was almost black. The only think keeping my upright is knowing that when I walk out of here, she will be walking beside me.

Without warning the woman had sheared along the entire left side of Magnus' body, snapping away 4 of his ribs to gain access to his heart. I closed my eyes and covered my ears, unfortunately my actions were not quick enough. The sound had already tore through my ear drums. I clenched my teeth together and voluntarily turned my back on Eva's body for the first time. I felt Hedwinn's hand on my shoulder, all I could hear was the snipping, cutting and eventual tearing of flesh. A hell bound Magnus took his last breath. I kept waiting for Eva to take hers.

Nothing, still nothing, not a peep. Reluctantly I turned back around, his body now covered with a grey sheet drenched in blood. The stench of it forced me to start throwing up violently into a bucket. Eva's body began to quiver and convulse as Katrina smashed Magnus' and Julia's pendants. Removing the light from within them.

The yellow light was an insanely bright firefly, the woman crushed the stone along with several molecules she wouldn't allow me to see. The woman had disembowelled Magnus and now she turned her attention to Eva. So much of his body's resources were now being flushed into hers, pieces of his heart, corneas, ligaments and pints of his blood were being exchanged. I couldn't watch.

Completely sickened by the sight of the ritual, the wall could no longer offer support as I fell unconscious to the floor.

S L Dixon

Printed in Great Britain
by Amazon.co.uk, Ltd.,
Marston Gate.